The Adventure of
The Spanish Drums

Martin Daley

First published in 2003 by BOOKCASE
This completely revised edition first published in 2010 by
The Irregular Special Press,
for Baker Street Studios Ltd,
Endeavour House,
170 Woodland Road, Sawston,
Cambridge, CB22 3DX, UK.

ISBN: 1-901091-43-0 (10 digit)
ISBN: 978-1-901091-43-4 (13 digit)

Cover Design: Antony J. Richards.

Cover Illustration: The Arroyo Drums.

Typeset in 8/11/20pt Palatino

For my Parents – fifty not out

Acknowledgement

Unfortunately, on this occasion, Mr. Sydney Paget was unable to provide some of his marvellous drawings that so often enhance the published cases of my friend.

Shortly before publication of this adventure, therefore, I contacted Inspector Armstrong of the Cumberland Constabulary to ask if he could provide me with some photographs from the period. Not only did he do so (with the help of some of his local contacts) he even supplied me with some actual pictures taken by the local press during and shortly after our investigation.

I owe a great deal of thanks therefore, not only to the Inspector but to the Carlisle Library; to Mr Phil Evans who specialises in photographs from the period; and to Mr. Stuart Eastwood of the Military Museum at Carlisle Castle, as well as other local historians, all of whom gave their permission for their pictures to be used.

I would also like to express my thanks to my fellow medical practitioner, Dr. Christophe Vever for reading the manuscript of this adventure and correcting any errors.

JOHN H. WATSON MD.

[Carlisle Castle Gateway on Arroyo Day, 1911]

Chapter One

A Brief Military Career

It was during late summer in the final year of that atrocious war when my domestic circumstances allowed me to visit my old friend Mr. Sherlock Holmes at his apiary hideaway in Sussex.

Having rejoined my old regiment at the start of the war I had completed my medical duties at Netley some months earlier and was once more settling down into civilian life. My practice was buoyant and I was spending a lot of my leisure time writing up some of the many cases I had been involved in with my friend.

Holmes of course had served his country with distinction, during the two years leading up to this latest conflict, when he successfully dealt with the Von Bork affair; bringing the matter to its conclusion as the opening salvos sounded, immediately prior to our entry into the disastrous war, in August of 1914. I had not seen my old friend since his dealings with the German spy and was looking forward to meeting up with him again, not to mention anticipating a relaxing rural break.

Upon my arrival Holmes gave me a warm, unfussy welcome to his villa. After a few days of drinking in the fresh coastal air, I certainly came to realise why Holmes chose this lifestyle, which was as far removed from his adventurous years based in the capital, as could be imagined. The dwelling itself was situated on the southern slopes of the Downs and afforded breathtaking views over the Channel. My friend and I spent our time chatting about old times and taking walks along the coastline and down the particularly treacherous path – almost vertical in places – to the pebbled beach below.

It was one morning during my stay that prompted my account of the following adventure. I was normally a late riser but the beautifully sunny morning in question found me freshening up; having returned from my walk to the nearby village of Fulworth, where I had bought a newspaper. Martha, Holmes" housekeeper, had made breakfast and I joined my friend on the patio to enjoy our leisurely, yet substantial meal.

We chatted idly before I picked up the paper to read. After a while my concentration started to drift to times past. Staring absentmindedly out to sea, my thoughts were mischievously interrupted by Holmes.

"Ah! My dear fellow, I see you are thinking back to our Cumberland adventure."

For a split second I was incredulous. "How on earth ..." I started, and suddenly realised that Holmes had been observing me for some moments. Before I could recover the situation by attempting to follow Holmes's methods, my old friend pressed home his advantage over me by explaining his line of reasoning.

"I observed you reading the morning paper and noticed your gaze as it aimlessly drifted from the written page. Seeing that the page in question details the latest casualties from the front and having read the piece myself as you prepared your toilet, I regarded the column on the senior officers that detailed the loss of, amongst others, the gallant Captain – or should I say, noting his field commission – Major George Armstrong, of the Border Regiment. It was clear to me that you had also read of the loss of that fine officer and as such, I deduce that your mind has taken you back to our adventure in that northerly county all those years ago."

Holmes was quite correct in his deductions of course, as my expression clearly betrayed my genuine sadness as I read of the loss of Major Armstrong, whom I had last met when he was a junior Lieutenant, some years earlier.

The piece detailed his seeing action in Northern Europe with his regiment, at the first two battles at Ypres and the Somme, where he not only received his field commission to major but was also commended for the Military Cross. It concluded by stating that he had fallen at Cambrai.

"Incidentally," added Holmes, again interrupting my brown study, "I am surprised you have not dug the case out of your considerable pile and recounted the adventure to our adoring public."

I knew with this last comment he was teasing me unnecessarily and I must confess to being a little piqued at his cruelty. "I simply haven't got round to listing that particular adventure yet," I blustered, without much conviction.

"Seriously," he went on, "I do believe the case is worth chronicling. I feel you would also find it a cathartic experience, Watson, as I have always sensed you have been troubled by your military experiences."

Notwithstanding my recent war efforts, there was more than an element of truth in his summation and his comments stayed with me for the following few days. On the journey home therefore, I decided to act on Holmes's advise.

That evening I went to my study and opened my old despatch box, in which I stored the yet to be published cases of my friend. As I dug down into the box, moving bundles of papers out of the way in so doing, the hairs on the back of my neck stood on end as I came to the object of my search. At the bottom of the box was a bundle with two words on the cover sheet that were slightly obscured by the black ribbon that held the file together. By simply untying the bundle, it was as if some psychological switch was tripped and my mind was instantly filled with the adventure that took us to the far north-western corner of England in that unforgettable October of 1903.

In recounting this tale, it occurs to me that this was one of the few occasions when I myself, introduced an investigation to the great consulting detective. The two investigations I directly brought to him were the adventure involving the hydraulic engineer, Mr. Victor Hatherley and that of Colonel Warburton's madness. Then there were the two other mysteries that resulted from letters I received from former acquaintances; the first from my old school friend 'Tadpole' Phelps that I recounted under the title *The Naval Treaty* and the second, which I am about to relate here. A letter also activated this case – this time received from an old army colleague.

It has never been my intention through the publication of my humble scribblings to produce an autobiographical account of my life to date, but perhaps, dear reader, you will allow me a few pages to elaborate on the snippets I have given you so far of my army career. This request is made as I feel the illustration of how bonds between men established in times of great adversity has a direct bearing on the case in question.

*****

As the New Year of 1879 dawned, I had completed a year as House Surgeon at Bart's and was wrestling with the difficult decision regarding my future career prospects. The layered structure of medical personnel within the hospital was such that a doctor in his mid twenties, such as I, would probably have to wait a further twenty years before picking up a senior position. This thought did not particularly inspire me, yet I did not have the capital to set up practice on my own.

It was one morning in the February of the New Year that the thought of a career in the army first occurred to me. I was reading the newspaper when my eye fell upon the account of the slaughter at Isandlwana and the subsequent heroics at Roake's Drift later that day, during the – then current – war with the Zulus. I was intrigued by the roles played by Lieutenants Chard and Bromhead, and particularly that of Surgeon Major Reynolds, during the second of the two actions. The report stated that Reynolds – who was in charge of the field hospital at the camp '... attended imperturbably to the wounded during the ferocious assault'. The fact that the piece concentrated mainly on the latter victorious and honourable battle, rather than the humiliating defeat of the former, did not occur to me at the time.

The three officers mentioned, along with eight of their colleagues would receive Victoria Crosses later that year for their efforts in attempting to repel the Zulu army that outnumbered the British forces almost forty-to-one.

Knowing that we were also fighting a war in Afghanistan at the same time, the thought struck me that not only would there be perhaps a greater chance of promotion in the medical corps but the opportunity of travel and adventure would also present itself.

During the following months I made further enquiries and gave the matter serious consideration. I discovered that an army assistant surgeon earned £200 a year, with his keep and living quarters provided. It occurred to me that after ten years' service, I could retire on half pay with enough money saved to set myself up in private practice. As a military career promised these advantages to a medical man, my mind was made up I decided to apply to The Army Medical School, which was part of the Royal Victoria Hospital at Netley in Hampshire.

The reply to my application was my first, albeit minor, setback. I was informed that I had missed the opening course of the year that commenced in March and would have to wait until the second course that was to begin in October. I did in the meantime however, pass the entrance examination and looked forward to the autumn when I would be enrolled into the British Army.

When the time came, I enjoyed my training and the environment enormously. Queen Victoria had laid the foundation stone to the hospital in May 1856 and The Army Medical School moved there from Chatham later that same year. It was the perfect location for such a facility, facing, as it did, Southampton Water. The long pier that jutted out from the hospital allowed invalids coming from far off campaigns to be transported virtually to the entrance, although some had to be transferred on to our own vessel, the *Florence Nightingale,* as the heavy troop ships were too heavy for the shallow waters around the pier.

The grounds of the hospital and the surrounding areas were beautiful and I enjoyed many a long walk, savouring the tranquillity. Near the pier stood an imitation medieval cross, in memory of comrades lost in the Crimean War. I regularly stood looking at the memorial and thinking what adventures lay ahead of me.

Our medical studies included learning about various diseases we would encounter throughout the Empire, along with the treatment of wounds from different weapons, preventative medicine and practical organisation of military hospitals. As well as all this we were left in no doubt that Netley was a military environment; candidates were required to wear uniform and attend parades.

I passed my final exam in February 1880 and became Lieutenant John H. Watson, Assistant Army Surgeon, something I immensely proud of at the time. As I have detailed elsewhere, less than a month after passing my final examination, I was posted to India where I was to join my allocated regiment, the Fifth Northumberland Fusiliers, who were already serving there. I arrived in Bombay in the April of that year.

Having my mind set on joining the Northumbrians and having read up on the regimental history during my journey, I was surprised and a little disappointed to learn after only a month that I was to be transferred to the Berkshires, who were serving in Afghanistan and who, I was told, were short of medical staff.

I was therefore, along with some other recently arrived officers, sent by steamer to Karachi and then by rail to Sibi and finally by camel over the mountains and across the border to the strategically important town of Kandahar to join my new regiment – the 66th Berkshire Regiment of Foot. It was during this journey that I first encountered Colonel Hayter, with whom I remained friends after we both left the army.

Kandahar itself had been taken earlier in the war and the garrison we were bolstering, was defended by both British regular soldiers and Indian sepoys, drawn from the 1st Bombay Native Infantry, Jacob's Horse and, of course, my own new regiment.

It was now the early summer of 1880 and the bloody war had raged for almost two years. Afghanistan was a desolate region of high mountains and barren plains, inhabited by fierce Muslim tribesmen who controlled the country by guarding the endless mountain passes across the North West Frontier. As far as the Afghans were concerned, they were fighting a *jihad*; a word I learned that meant 'holy war', against whom they saw as the infidels – the none believers.

Upon our arrival at the cantonment we discovered that – despite their defeat at Kabul – 20,000 tribesmen led by Ayub Khan were advancing towards Kandahar. Early on the morning of 27th July 1880 – a date imprinted on my mind forever – Brigadier General George Burrows led our forces out to meet them. The two armies met on a hot dusty plain at the village of Maiwand, fifty miles north west of our garrison.

Taking advantage of the familiar terrain, the enemy moved forward, while their artillery bombarded our rear, where casualties were as heavy as those in the front lines. The noise and the pressure waves from the constant bombardment were at times unbearable. Hundreds of our men were lost; some hacked to pieces before my very eyes – a fearful sight.

The fighting was so fierce that I saw a stretcher-bearer lose an arm as he moved to help a fallen comrade. After that incident, his colleagues dared not break cover to collect the wounded. Even now, many years later as I write this account, my blood runs cold at some of the scenes I witnessed on that awful day.

A young lad was brought to me for attention at one point. Although conscious, he was clearly mortally wounded with severe head injuries; black scorch marks circled two terrible head wounds and his thick brown hair was matted crimson by the blood that oozed from them. Very rarely has a day passed since that dreadful hour when I have not thought of

13

that poor boy's expression; his eyes filled with a mixture of fear and hope that I could perform some miracle for him.

My mind was racing at this point; my life flashing before me in this moment of intense stress. I thought of the brave Surgeon Major Reynolds, who had partly inspired me to join the army, less than eighteen short months earlier. Far from the rejoicing of victory in newspaper reports however, I was now realising that there was no honour *or* glory in this butchery.

It was as I was attending to the young soldier that I was lifted off my feet and sent reeling. Prone, I instinctively reached up to quell the searing pain I felt in my shoulder. I later discovered that I had taken a bullet that had been shot by a *Jezzailchi* – a marksman skilled in the use of his immensely long barrelled rifle. I make no apology for repeating that I owe my life to the prompt actions of my orderly Murray who loaded me onto the back of a packhorse, prior to joining the retreat to Kandahar.

This withdrawal however, was equally as treacherous and as terrifying as the battle itself. As we made our way through the flinty mountain passes, more Jezails – fired from the ledges above – cracked and popped around us. The Afghan guerrillas worked in perfect unison against us; no sooner had the *Jezzailchis* ceased firing above us, then their colleagues would appear like genies from behind the rocks that lined the mountain passes.

These tribesmen were an even more fearful sight closer up; with their bearded faces and dressed as they were in their baggy garb, while their spiked helmets were clearly visible under their *Puggarree*. As they ran towards us wielding their long Khyber knives above their heads, the triumphalistic screeching war cry they emitted was enough to curdle the blood of the bravest soldier. How we managed to extricate ourselves from such a hopeless situation, especially as I was so debilitated, I am not entirely sure.

Lieutenant General James Primrose was in charge of the Kandahar garrison and he decided to defend the whole of the perimeter. Breaches in the walls were repaired and gun emplacements were set up. As we approached relative safety, we were subjected to a further assault by, what seemed to be, an endless group of ferocious Ghazi warriors. It was during this final skirmish that I apparently passed out with exhaustion.

It was several hours later that I found myself coming out of my deep state of unconsciousness in the comfort of a hospital bed. It was such an awakening that I wanted to last for ever, such was my relief at obviously making it safely back to the interior of the fort – wounded but otherwise whole. Even as I moved, and was instantly reminded of the wound in my shoulder, as well as a further – hitherto unknown – injury in the calf of my leg, I felt safe and content in the confines of the garrison.

There was faint rustling sound of a punkah fan overhead and I finally opened my eyes to find two figures standing at the foot of my bed. One was my faithful orderly, to whom I shall be eternally indebted. The other was a tall, handsome, fair-haired officer, who Murray introduced as Subaltern Harry Vaughan. He went on to explain that it was the young Subaltern who led a group of soldiers out from behind the lines, in an effort to drive off the rebels. Had he not done so, Murray, myself, and the others would have surely been done for.

Mercifully, I discovered that we did not receive any further casualties during this final assault but I was later given to understand that Subaltern Vaughan's actions were rather frowned upon by his superior officers. They viewed his charge out from behind the lines as being rather rash and more likely to endanger further loss. I must confess that Murray and I did not share this view however, and we both informed him of our gratitude for his actions.

The whole of the August that followed saw us besieged in the garrison by Ayub Khan, before we were finally relieved by Major General Frederick 'Bobs' Roberts who marched over 300 miles across the mountains from Kabul, with his relieving army of ten thousand men.

Subaltern Vaughan was then given the task of supervising the transportation of the wounded, myself included, back across the border to Peshawur, where I was to continue my convalescence. Our caravan wove its way between the dangerous hills and jagged peaks of central Afghanistan; with its stony defiles that were like baking ovens. Although the camels – with their large flat feet – coped with the terrain, I remember the poor ponies constantly slipping on the flinty surfaces.

It was as we were coming down one of these treacherous mountain paths, that Vaughan had cause to display further gallantry. I heard one of the sepoys shout back, '*Huzoor Vaughan*! Gilzais scouts ahead'. I looked out of my wagon and was horrified to see a group of local tribesmen blocking the road at the foot of the pass. My immediate thought was that we were all to be slaughtered after all.

Vaughan however, calmly rode ahead to meet the leader of the group. He was an exotic figure; someone who could have been taken from the pages of an Eastern fairytale, such were his outlandish clothes. He sat astride his Afghan pony in his loose fitting robes and pyjama-type trousers, over which he wore a long, elaborately coloured coat. Black ringlets of hair protruded from underneath his green turban. My attention however, was almost immediately drawn to the long barrel of his Jezail rifle that was slung over his shoulder, and the vicious looking Khyber knife that hung from his belt.

Vaughan, quite calmly, spoke to the leader in his own tongue, for a few minutes and to my utter astonishment, the latter retreated back to his group and ushered them out of the way, thus allowing us to pass through unmolested. Once through the labyrinth of passes, we were out onto the sun-scorched plains.

I recovered enough during this period to hold several conversations with the young officer. I began by complimenting him on the way he handled the potentially dangerous situation at the pass. He explained modestly that he simply pointed out to the scout that we were a group of harmless wounded who posed no threat to them. Being a relatively small scouting group they did not wish to engage in combat either. I must say I was not only impressed by his bravery but also his coolness.

It transpired that he was related on his mother's side, to Lennard Stokes, my old rugby captain at Blackheath, who went on to win twelve caps for England. Stokes was a fellow medical student; he studied at Guy's whilst I was at Bart's. It seemed bizarre discussing with Vaughan the merits of the best drop kicker in the game of Rugby Football, on those dusty Afghan plains but I could not help being drawn to this man, who's bravery and ambition epitomised everything that I thought good about the British soldier. He informed me at one point that he expected to leave the Berkshires in the near future, in an effort to further his career with another regiment. I recall him telling me that he hoped the army re-organisation that was due to take place within the next couple of years would provide him with the opportunity for advancement. His dilemma was whether to stay on the sub continent and apply for a position with one of the regiments out there, or return to England and seek promotion in one of the home based regiments.

We arrived safely at Peshawur and I wished Vaughan farewell, thanking him once more for saving my life. If I thought my problems were over upon our arrival at Peshawur however, I was to be mistaken, as the enteric fever I contracted, compounded my problems. By October of the same year I was back in Bombay where the medical board decreed that I should be sent home to England immediately.

We sailed for Portsmouth at the end of the month and called at Malta in mid-November. I was one of twenty or so invalids, who found themselves on English soil again on the afternoon of Friday 26th November. Looking back at this almost forty years on, I can see a certain irony, given that twelve months after I entered Netley, full of ambition and a sense of adventure, I was now being transferred back there – this time as a patient. The building I had first viewed as a breeding ground for some of the army's finest now appeared a grey and unwelcoming place.

Readers familiar with my writings will know that shortly thereafter I was awarded a pension of eleven shillings and sixpence a day, after being invalided out of the army. It was then that I moved back up to London where I was to become acquainted with another man who was to have a profound influence on my life.

Mr. Sherlock Holmes provided the escapism and camaraderie I had been denied due to my all too brief military career and through the adventures I shared with him, the bitterness I initially felt after being discharged subsided as the years past. Almost a quarter of a century later, I was destined to bring valued friends and colleagues from two different worlds together.

Chapter Two

Journey To The North

Holmes had some weeks earlier completed the investigation involving Professor Presbury and I had my – by now blossoming – practice in Queen Anne Street. It was late afternoon on the second Monday of October in the year 1903, when I returned to my surgery after being called away earlier in the day. As I entered I found a letter addressed to myself 'c/o 221B Baker Street'. The maid explained that Mrs. Hudson had sent Billy round with it that morning. Upon opening it I was amazed to find that it was from none other than my old saviour from Afghanistan, Subaltern – now Captain – Harry Vaughan.

I regret to say that I had gradually lost touch with Vaughan, Murray and many others of my brave colleagues, but now here was one of those characters from the past writing to me over twenty years later. The letter ran thus:

Dear Watson,

I hope you can remember your former colleague Harry Vaughan from Afghanistan. I am aware of your friendship with Mr. Sherlock Holmes through your publications in *The Strand* magazine. I am writing in the hope that we can commission the services of Mr. Holmes in a most serious and embarrassing problem for the regiment. Our most treasured trophy from our many campaigns, The Arroyo Drums, has been stolen! Please wire as soon as possible if you and your friend are able to help.

Yours etc.

Captain H Vaughan
Border Regiment

So old Harry did leave the Berkshires after all, I thought to myself.

Although, as I stated earlier, my own experiences of the army left me somewhat troubled, paradoxically my interest and enthusiasm for military matters remained undiminished. I was therefore intrigued by the letter, not only as it was sent by my former colleague but because of the hastily referred to drums; the subject of the narrative. My natural reaction was to refer to my not inconsiderable collection of military history books. After a brief search I found the subject that was causing such consternation.

I learned that the trophies were the spoils of a victory won at the northern Spanish village of Arroyo dos Molinos during the Peninsular War in 1811. The Borders – then the 34th (Cumberland) Regiment – were part of Sir Rowland Hill's Division who surprised a French Division by a series of marches *to*, and a dawn attack *on* the village.

While the main body of the Division attacked the village, the 34th were sent to cut off the French retreat. By coincidence they came up against the French 34th Infantry Regiment of the Line. Heavily outnumbered by the great phalanx of Napoleon's Infantry during the skirmish that followed, the Cumberland Regiment not only overcome their adversaries but Sergeant Moses Simpson wrenched the French Drum

Major's mace from him and the six French drums were also captured together with most of the Regiment. The Border Regiment thereafter were accorded the right to wear the red and white pom-pom of the French 34th on their shakos and in 1845 Queen Victoria assented to award the Battle Honour of Arroyo dos Molinos to the regiment.

[*The Arroyo Drums are the Border Regiment's most prized trophies*]

I read with continued fascination that in their long history and the many campaigns they have served in, The Arroyo Drums remain the Border Regiment's most prized trophies; gained as they were from one of their most successful victories. As a footnote to the piece I was examining, it was stated that every year on the anniversary of the battle, the regiment celebrates 'Arroyo Day'. The drums are paraded in period uniform in the square of Carlisle Castle. 'Arroyo Day' was celebrated every 28th October!

What a magnificent story, I thought. With great enthusiasm I related the tale, the letter from my military colleague and our past experiences to my wife, who, reaching for my hat and coat, suggested I take the note back to 221B and consult Mr. Sherlock Holmes without further delay.

It was a cold evening, in keeping with the time of year, and the gunmetal skies were lowering menacingly over Baker Street as I approached my former lodgings. It was with the usual mixture of eagerness, anticipation and a small feeling of dread, that I rang the bell of 221B, as I could never be sure in what disposition I would find my friend.

Mrs. Hudson greeted me warmly as the door, "Doctor, what a pleasant surprise! Did you get the letter I sent round this morning?"

"I did thank you, Mrs. Hudson. It is regarding the letter I have come to visit Mr. Holmes."

"Go straight up, Doctor," she said taking my hat and coat, "you will find him in a jovial mood."

The good housekeeper's appraisal of my old friend's mood proved accurate; I had barely crossed the landing and was about to put my hand on the knob of our sitting room door when his familiar voice bellowed out, "Friend Watson!"

As I entered, the warmth of the welcoming fire that blazed away from behind the familiar grate immediately engulfed me. Holmes himself was standing on the hearthrug in his mouse coloured dressing gown. He was in the process of tossing a glowing coal back into the fire with the tongs, after lighting his pipe. He gestured me to take my old seat. "Your step on the well-trodden staircase is unmistakable. What brings you out on this chill evening? Will you stay for supper?"

A jovial mood indeed, I thought. "Good evening old fellow," I said moving towards the welcoming fire, "it's not a social call Holmes – it is business. I received a letter from an old army colleague, only this afternoon. He wants your help."

I briefly explained my relationship with Vaughan and handed over his correspondence to Holmes. The detective sucked on his cherrywood pipe and studied the envelope and its contents in his usual thorough manner.

"Carlisle, indeed!" he said at last. "Never having been to that most northern of English cities, this is the second time in as many months that it has been brought to my attention." He did not elaborate on this curious comment, but continued to devour the contents of the letter. "An interesting, yet brief message," he mumbled, tapping the letter with the long stem of his pipe. I concluded that my friend never ceased to amaze me as he casually announced, "We shall take the eight seventeen out of Euston and head for the city of Carlisle, in the county of Cumberland tomorrow."

Having originally felt that Holmes would neither be interested in a military problem, nor be receptive to a long journey I was taken aback and found myself protesting at the short notice, "What about my wife? My Practice?" I said.

"My dear fellow, your old colleague and saviour needs our help. 'Arroyo Day' is a mere three weeks away!" – there was more than a hint of sarcasm in Holmes's tone, as he did not share my enthusiasm for the military – "we cannot possibly refuse. I suggest you send your friend a telegram advising him of our intentions."

"Of course," I agreed after a moment's thought. "I shall have to skip supper however, as I will need to make the necessary arrangements."

After agreeing to meet at the station the following morning, I took my leave and headed for the post office on the corner of Torrington Square, with the intention of sending a telegram north, prior to my returning home.

I must confess to approaching the latter of these two tasks rather sheepishly, as I knew that for the second time within a month I would be asking my dear wife's permission to leave her for a few days, while I accompanied Holmes on another investigation. Furthermore I knew I would have to impose on my neighbour Jackson once more, to act as locum for my thriving business.

I need not have fretted as my wife assented without hesitation to my few days away. I am sure she viewed Holmes and I as two schoolboys who never quite grew up, and she was always loathed to spoil our fun. Similarly, Jackson was equally obliging. How fortunate it was, I thought to myself afterwards, that his surgery is in close proximity to my own.

So it was with great enthusiasm that night that I packed a case, anticipating not only the adventure that lay ahead and my first visit to Cumberland, but of my meeting up once more with my old military colleague Harry Vaughan.

At the appointed hour on the following, fresh autumnal morning, I found myself walking along the platform looking for the appropriate carriage. Holmes leaned out of one of the windows some way down the train, "Good morning Watson! A beautiful day for a train journey through the Lake District!"

"Indeed," I agreed, climbing aboard.

Our long journey commenced in fairly uneventful fashion. I whiled away the first few hours by reading the newspaper and inevitably thinking about military matters; my brief but eventful career and some of the characters I encountered. For his part Holmes divided his time between calculating the speed of the train and the distance travelled, and quietly meditating in that familiar semi-conscious state.

As the train crossed the county border into Cumberland, my companion suddenly became alert, as if smelling the impending case ahead. "So Watson, tell me more about this friend and former colleague of yours."

"A fine man Holmes; honourable, ambitious and brave as a lion. I'm only sorry I did not have more time to spend with him." I continued by repeating to Holmes in more detail the series of events that led to our paths crossing all those years ago, in that far corner of the Empire.

As we progressed further north I gradually became aware of the drop in temperature. In fact, by the time we reached Carlisle, on the stroke of four o'clock, I would estimate it was several degrees below that when we had left in the capital that morning. It was the first time I had visited the Border City and I stepped down from the train quite excited about the adventure that lay ahead; the new surroundings, catching up with my old colleague and the military background to our visit. I spotted the Border Regiment Captain himself, along the platform; his tall, square build and unmistakable shock of fair hair distinguishing him from the crowd.

[Unknown to Holmes and myself, we were captured in this photograph as we left the train]

"My dear fellow," I said, approaching him, "it is wonderful to see you again, you haven't changed a bit since I saw you last." The comment was a genuine one; save for the fleck of grey amongst the blond hair around the temples, Vaughan was exactly how I remembered him.

"It is kind of you to say so Watson," he replied, "it is over twenty years since our Afghan campaign."

"May I introduce my friend Mr. Sherlock Holmes," I said.

"Mr. Holmes, I'm delighted to meet you," said Vaughan, reaching out his hand. "It is very kind of you to come and help us at such short notice. I am aware of several of your cases through the writings of our mutual friend."

"Watson does tend to glorify our little adventures," replied the detective, "we shall simply do our best."

Vaughan led us out onto the street where he had a four-wheeler waiting to take us the relatively short journey to our lodgings. We had barely driven one hundred yards up the slight incline outside the station and through the twin drum bastion towers, Vaughan referred to as "The Citadel", when our attention was caught by some commotion on the street outside. As we looked out from our carriage, I saw an unusual public house. The striking feature about the tall establishment was the curved, elongated shape of the building itself. It did not posses, as most buildings do, a normal gable end, but had a distinctive semi circular extremity, that gave the building great character. The entrance to the Inn, which jutted out into the street, was at the centre point of this semi circle. The cause of the commotion was the handful of brutish looking characters that – having spilled out onto the pavement – were scuffling between themselves.

"They are starting early tonight," said Vaughan. Following my gaze towards the Inn and the high walls beyond it, he continued, "That's the County Gaol; the pub is the City Arms," he said pointing to the magnificent coat of arms and the Prince of Wales feathers that stood atop the building. "It is commonly known as the 'Gaol Tap'. You do not want to being hanging around there after dark, my friend."

"No, I could well imagine," I murmured.

*[The twin drum bastion towers of the Citadel
opposite the station]*

Although it was by now late afternoon, I felt Holmes
would want to initiate his investigations immediately, but as
we drew up to the entrance of our digs, he surprised me by
turning to the army officer and stating, "I suggest we get a
good night's rest and then look into your little problem
tomorrow."

"As you wish," said Vaughan. "I have some unfinished
paperwork at the castle, I will leave you to settle in and join
you for dinner later – say eight o'clock?" Then turning to me
he reached out his hand once more and said, "It really is good
to see you again Watson."

The accommodation Vaughan had arranged for us was
right in the heart of the city opposite the town hall. The
Crown and Mitre Inn and Coffee House appeared at first
glance to be a fairly basic establishment, but it was one that
would prove to be both comfortable and convenient. We

entered to be greeted by a short squat man with a ruddy complexion. "Good afternoon gentlemen," he said pleasantly, "I'm Sam Graham, I run the 'Mitre' wid me wife Mary."

"Good afternoon Mr. Graham," said Holmes, "I see you have your own little corner of violin land!" Holmes was looking past our host to two plaques that were behind him on the wall. One referred to Sir Walter Scott as having stayed in the establishment before marrying his Carlisle born wife, in 1797. The one Holmes was referring to, however, was the one next to it, which stated that the great Niccolo Paginini had both stayed at the Inn and performed there in September 1833. I understood Holmes's comment, as the virtuoso violinist and composer was one the masters of his favourite instrument whom he so admired.

"Yes, our small claim to fame," said Graham following our gaze with a smile. "I hope you enjoy your stay gentlemen. Anythin' ye need, just give us a shout. I'll get the lad to tek ye bags."

As if by magic a young chap of about nine years of age appeared at our side and proceeded to gamely load our bags onto his back as if he were some kind of packhorse. He made a comical sight as he attempted to climb the stairs to the upper floors and Holmes and I could not stop ourselves from relieving the young chap of some of his baggage. A talkative young chap he turned out to be, with his father's dialect already taking a strong hold. He took great delight in telling us about how the Inn was due to be demolished and rebuilt next year as "... the county's top hotel!"

We climbed two flights of stairs before arriving at our rooms. The owner's son opened the door and struggled through. As he deposited our luggage in the centre of the floor, I held out half a crown as reward for his sterling efforts. The little tyke's arm shot out and back like a serpent's tongue, taking the coin as quick as you like.

"Thank you sir," he said disappearing back down the stairs, in search of his next assignment.

Our rooms were basic but adequate for our purposes. We had a sitting room at the northern corner of the Inn with two separate bedrooms off it, making our suite a natural 'L' shape. The main room featured an ornate fireplace, a mixture of comfortable chairs, a chez-long, a writing bureau and a magnificent – if a little neglected – grandfather clock that laboriously ticked the hours away.

The room not only overlooked English Street on one side, but there was evidence to substantiate the young lad's claim about the demolition work on the northern side of the Inn. The buildings next to it had been razed to the ground and this afforded us magnificent views of both the Cathedral, which was now the next building to the Inn, and further down Castle Street to the magnificent 11th century structure itself.

We unpacked our few belongings and it was only after sitting down to enjoy a pipe that a great feeling of lassitude caught up on me after our long journey. I must confess at that point to being relieved that Holmes had made his earlier suggestion about the commencement of our investigation. Having said that, I was looking forward to spending a couple of hours with my old comrade over dinner.

After freshening up, Holmes and I went down to what could scarcely pass as the dining room a little after seven thirty. Harry met us shortly thereafter and we both immediately launched into reciting tales of our times together and our two subsequent careers. I was enthralled about his military exploits. Vaughan explained that after I left him in Peshawur, he served out the following few months of the war to its close in late 1880.

"Under the Cardwell reforms of 1881," he continued, "it was dictated that each regiment must have two battalions, one serving at home, which would act as reinforcement for the other, which would serve overseas. Thus the 34th Cumberland and the 55th Westmorland were joined as the 1st and 2nd Battalions of the Border Regiment; I took a chance and joined the Battalion in India.

"In '94 we took part in operations against the tribesmen on the North West Frontier in Waziristan – fierce fighters the old Waziris," he reflected.

"Four years ago we were in Malta, on our way home from India when the Great War against the Boers broke out. We were sent directly to South Africa and became one of the first reinforcements to the garrison. We joined the army of Sir Redvers Buller in Natal and fought in all the battles, whilst attempting to raise the siege of Ladysmith."

I could see the sparkle in his eye as he leaned forward with excitement telling me of the various skirmishes he had taken part in with his friend and colleague Sergeant George 'Geordie' Armstrong. "You'll meet him tomorrow, by the way. Perhaps our finest hour came at Bushman's Kop," he continued, using the condiments and cutlery on the table to illustrate the set-piece battle and support his narrative.

"We were camped about three miles from the Kop with the Somersets and the Irish Rifles with support from the Royal Artillery's 15 pounders, who bombarded the enemy positions. The Irish joined us in attacking on the right flank in two lines. The firing was ferocious, with bullets and pom-pom shells sweeping over their positions.

"I must confess to being a little impetuous at times and, spurred on by my fiery subordinates; I led the lads into the open, where we were pretty exposed at one point. Geordie, who acts as the voice on my shoulder in such situations, and who was initially was against the advance, advised that our only option was to push on. So I led the lads in another advance and we secured victory shortly afterwards. What a triumph! Yes old Armstrong and Vaughan showed Johnny Boer a thing or two," he concluded, with obvious pride.

It was times like these – listening to soldiers like Harry Vaughan – that I regretted not having experienced a longer military career myself. I was in my element, revelling in the tales as if I were there myself, whilst at the same time recognising through my own experience, the horror of such situations. I could not get enough of his military exploits and I must confess that in all of my excitement, I almost forgot about Holmes's presence. He had been sitting quietly the whole evening, mulling over the odd cigarette.

At the end of the evening, we bade Captain Vaughan goodnight, arranging to meet him and his commanding officer at eight thirty the following morning, prior to finally commencing the investigation. On the way up to our rooms I felt obliged to apologise to Holmes, as I felt I had ignored him for most of the evening.

"Not at all Watson, do not trouble yourself," he said. "Like you I found the evening extremely interesting."

Chapter Three

The Problem

Our first full day in Carlisle saw us rise, break our fast and set off on the short walk to the castle. It was a bitterly cold morning, with a knee high ground mist covering the city centre. It did however, contribute to the freshness of the air, which was in marked contrast to the almost yellow, sometimes oily, fogs that frequently enveloped London and in doing so, provided its inhabitants with a rather poisonous atmosphere.

As we walked along Castle Street towards the castle itself and the river beyond, the mist became rather more dense and the medieval structure appeared as though it were rising out of an ice field; truly a breathtaking sight.

We approached the sentries on guard duty, who appeared more intent on confrontation, rather than welcome. Before we had time to explain our presence however, our companion from the previous night appeared, stood his colleagues down and took us under the portcullis, across the spacious square towards the Commanding Officer's Office on the first floor of one of the interior buildings. The castle itself was as impressive from the inside, as it appeared from the outside. One could sense its history in each corner.

Vaughan knocked and entered his superior's office. The spacious room had a large window that overlooked the castle square and was decorated with memorabilia from the regiment and its adventures; pictures of famous battles, portraits of previous commanding officers, models and a collection of books displayed in a beautiful oak panelled bookcase that lined one of the walls. As we entered, the Colonel rose from behind the large matching desk.

Lieutenant Colonel Richard Hulme DSO KCB was an imposing figure and a veteran of the North West Frontier and of the recent war in South Africa. He had commanded the regiment since its return from the Boer conflict.

Vaughan introduced us to his commanding officer, "Colonel, may I introduce Mr. Sherlock Holmes and his colleague Doctor John Watson."

"Gentlemen, thank you for coming to help us with this most serious of crimes. I trust your accommodation is adequate, as for your fee Mr. Holmes …"

"My professional charges are upon a fixed scale," interrupted the detective, "I do not vary them, save when I omit them completely."

I must confess to being both slightly embarrassed and a little amused by Holmes's tone, who was never one to feel beneath another, and to that of the colonel's discomfort, as he was clearly not used to being spoken to so sharply.

"Quite," mumbled the latter rather uncomfortably.

"Now," started Holmes, addressing the Commanding Officer, "I would like you to tell me the series of events that have led us to this point."

"I'm sure you know of the significance of these trophies Mr. Holmes."

Before Holmes could express further irritation at the continuing prevarication, I hastily interjected, "We are familiar with the background to the Arroyo Drums Colonel," I said, encouraging him to continue.

"The theft appears to have taken place around midnight on Tuesday of last week, whilst I was at the camp of the Westmorland and Cumberland Yeomanry near Penrith. It is customary for the Border Regiment's Commanding Officer to inspect the local Yeomanry at their annual camp," he explained. "Whilst we were away, one of the guards was knocked unconscious during sentry duty. It seemed like the action of ignorant thugs at the time; perhaps a gang of drunkards rolling out of one of the nearby pubs, until we discovered the drums were missing when we returned. We feel the two incidents must be linked – hence the theory about Tuesday."

"I sense that you are keeping something from me Colonel," said Holmes. "Can you explain how only one of the sentries was injured?"

The Commanding Officer assumed an expression that was a mixture of embarrassment and rage. As he looked at Vaughan he said, "It would appear that we only have one sentry on duty during the night; or that *was* the case until last week." It was clear that Holmes had touched a raw nerve and the unwritten practice that was apparently unknown to the regiment's senior officer had come back to haunt the individuals responsible for turning 'Nelson's eye' to the practice.

"Exactly how long were you away?" Holmes was clearly not interested in the rights and wrongs of regimental protocol.

"We left on Monday morning to join the camp that afternoon. We were there until Thursday afternoon."

"Who was in your party?"

"I was accompanied by Captain Vaughan and a unit under the command of Sergeant Armstrong."

"Who was left in charge of the depot?"

"Overall command was passed to Major Young, supported by the new Regimental Sergeant Major McCue, who has only been with us since 1ˢᵗ October after transferring from the Northumberland Fusiliers."

"Ah, my old regiment, before I joined the Berkshires," I commented, turning to Vaughan, and much to Holmes's annoyance.

"Tell me, Colonel Hulme," continued my friend, "what steps have been taken so far?"

"All leave has been cancelled until the Arroyo Drums are found," – Hulme made no attempt to hide his indignation – "we have searched the castle high and low without success."

"Have you notified the local police?"

"As a matter of course we did," interjected Vaughan, "but they claim to be particularly shorthanded at the moment and view this as a relatively minor issue. Inspector Armstrong is a fine officer – our own Sergeant's cousin incidentally – but he could only spare one of his plain clothed sergeants – Smith."

"And he hardly inspires confidence," added the colonel, "met with the fellow on Monday."

"It was for that reason that we initially preferred to keep it a regimental matter," resumed Captain Vaughan.

"And yet you have seen fit to consult myself." Holmes concluded.

"Time is now of the essence Mr. Holmes," it was the commanding officer again, "'Arroyo Day' is fast approaching." Holmes chuckled at, what seemed to him to be an insignificant matter. "We did not invite you here to amuse yourself at our expense Mr. Holmes." said the C.O. sharply.

"My apologies Colonel," – Holmes was smiling, yet contrite – "I am confident that we will solve the mystery in good time. With your permission I would like to spend some time inspecting the castle, but first I would like to interview your staff if I may."

"I am sure Captain Vaughan can make the necessary arrangements," said Colonel Hulme, somewhat placated. He then requested that we return to update him at "… sixteen hundred hours," that afternoon.

Vaughan took us from the Colonel's office, out on to the square and thence to an adjacent building where there was an office, he said, that could be used as an interview room. He informed us that we could not speak with Sergeant Armstrong as he was 'indisposed'. Furthermore, he added that the soldier who was on guard duty, and who was injured during the subsequent robbery was in the infirmary.

"I shall make a point of visiting him in hospital," said Holmes.

"He is still unconscious from his injuries," replied Vaughan.

"And his colleague who should have been on duty with him?"

"He is in the guardhouse. I will need the colonel's permission to release him."

"I will speak with the colonel again this afternoon on that issue."

The first member of the colonel's staff, Vaughan introduced us to therefore, was Lance Corporal Geoffrey Robins who, he informed us, acted as the commanding officer's secretary-cum-batman. The captain then excused himself to attend to his other duties. Robins was a slightly built, red headed man who, although in his thirtieth year retained a boyish appearance. Holmes began by simply asking Robins go through the events as he saw them.

"Well sir, the truth of it is that there is not a great deal to tell. The colonel and his party had left for Penrith on the Monday morning and all was quiet until Private Walker was discovered by his mate Nixon, who should have been on duty with him." Robins was clearly embarrassed by this last comment and I got the impression that everyone apart from the C.O. himself knew about the lax nocturnal security. That notwithstanding, Robins continued his account, "we were mystified as to the motive for the attack as nothing appeared to have been disturbed. It was not until the Thursday evening that it all added up. Captain Vaughan and I found that the old Frenchy's gear was missing when we went into the storage room. We were making the initial preparations for 'Arroyo Day', you see. You can imagine our feelings when we discovered the loss," he concluded, sadly.

"Where exactly was Walker found?"

"There is a toilet block just to the left as you come under the gate. He must have been on his way to visiting a place because he was found on the steps of the block."

"I think it more likely that he would have been returning to his post," said Holmes, cryptically.

"Anyway," resumed Robins who, like myself, did not seem to understand Holmes's comment, "as I said to Geordie

Armstrong; who took the drums and how, remains a mystery. It was then that your name was mentioned Mr. Holmes."

"I don't understand," said the detective.

"Well, Geordie and I were in the mess on Friday night, talking about the theft. I commented that we could do with your services. My older brother is in the Royal Mallows, you see, and I remember him telling me about how you solved the case involving Colonel Barclay back in "83.

"'Hang on a minute!' cries Geordie 'I'm sure old Vaughany knows his side-kick.'

"'Doctor Watson?' said I.

"'Yeah, that's right. I recall 'H' reading a copy of the magazine that his stories are in, and telling me that they were in Afghanistan together.'

"We then approached the colonel and Captain Vaughan, who got in touch with your good selves."

Clearly amused by the Lance Corporal's reference to myself as his 'side-kick', Holmes resumed his questioning.

"Where were the drums held?"

"As I say, we have a storage room in Queen Mary's Tower, across the square sir. All the regiment's trophies are kept there. I can show you if you like."

"That would be useful, but later. Finally Corporal, was anything else taken?"

"No sir," replied Robins.

"In that case I would like to speak with the Regimental Sergeant Major, if I may."

"I'll show him in sir."

"And Robins?" Holmes added as the Lance Corporal reached the door, "If you could wait outside and show us to the room from where the drums were stolen, it would be much appreciated." The young man nodded his assent and closed the door behind him.

Clearly Vaughan had asked the key personnel to make themselves available, as the RSM entered almost immediately. Standing over six feet tall, McCue was the archetypal Regimental Sergeant Major; with a ramrod straight back, dark slicked back hair with a matching handlebar moustache.

I, perhaps foolishly, tried to break the ice by referring to the fact that McCue and myself were both former members of the Northumberland Fusiliers.

"Really sir," said the RSM.

Holmes, as usual, had no inhibitions about questioning this rather intimidating figure.

"Where exactly were you when the drums were stolen?" he asked

"I don't know the exact time when the French drums and colours were stolen, sir. The general consensus appears to be that it was during the early hours of Tuesday morning, last week. If this is the case, I was here in my quarters."

"And Major Young?"

"To the best of my knowledge sir, Major Young spent every evening in the mess or in the officers' accommodation." I sensed some friction between the two, upon hearing this latest comment. The soldier continued in his broad north-eastern accent, "the only event that broke up the week was the discovering of the injured guard. I had expressed my reservations to Major Young previously but it was not until the incident that I ordered that the guards be doubled. It was not until the colonel's party returned that the true significance of the incident dawned."

"Were you aware of where the drums were held?" Holmes wanted to know.

"I couldn't have sworn to it before the furore sir. Although young Robins showed me round the castle when I arrived, the trophy room was not at the forefront of my mind."

"Thank you Regimental Sergeant Major McCue, that will be all," said my friend, concluding the short interview.

I found the senior NCO extremely difficult to read as, throughout the interview, he didn't give anything away; his face remained expressionless and his voice monotone. "Would you like me to ask Major Young to join you sir?" he asked as he got up to leave, "he is waiting outside."

"No, that will not be necessary," replied Holmes, "I do not believe he can tell us anything we have not heard already."

39

A moment later, after McCue had closed the door behind him, we heard raised voices outside the office. A figure I took to be Major Young not so much entered as burst in.

"Mr. Holmes? Which one of you is Mr. Holmes?"

"That is my pleasure," said my friend, "this is my friend and colleague Doctor Watson. Now you have us at a disadvantage," he added, knowing full well who he was addressing.

Ignoring me completely the man confirmed his identity, "I am Major Clive Young. What is this the RSM tells me – that you do not want to speak to me?"

"Oh, I do apologise Major, I did not realise you had some vital information that would help solve this mystery." There was more than a hint of sarcasm in Holmes's tone. This was however, lost on Young and once more I found myself amused at Holmes's attitude towards the rather senior military personnel.

"Vital information? Vital information? I was the officer in charge of the depot on the night of the theft," continued Young, unabashed.

"How long have you held your current rank?"

"Only since February of this year. Why do you ask?"

Holmes ignored the question. "And was this the first time you were left in charge in Colonel Hulme's absence?"

Suddenly it dawned on Young that he had dug a rather large hole for himself. His haughty air and arrogant tone instantly disappeared. "Well I wasn't personally on guard myself," he said, rather pathetically.

"No, but I wager that you were fully aware of the custom of one guard being on duty?" There was an uncomfortable silence. "I believe Private Walker was quite badly injured. Yet it was not until the Colonel's party returned later in the week, that the theft was discovered. Still I'm sure no one blames you personally Major," Holmes said, rather generously, "thank you for your time. If I need any further information from you, I know where to find you." Young left the room quietly. "Another one full of his own importance," sneered Holmes, after him.

"Quite an unusual pair," I said. "I got the impression that there wasn't much love lost between the two."

"I was certainly interested in the Regimental Sergeant Major," replied Holmes.

"Really? I thought he had all the personality of a brick!"

Chuckling at my comment, my friend then announced, "I think we have had quite enough talking for one morning Watson. I think it is now time to take up Robins's offer of inspecting the scene of the crime.

[The Captain's Tower, with one of the barrack blocks beyond]

The lance corporal took us across the large square and past a half-moon battery, apparently built toward the end of Henry VIII's reign, according to our guide. Holmes mumbled something under his breath, little interested in Robins's topic of conversation. The battery stood in front of a large stone curtain that protected the inner ward of the castle. We walked through the curtain's magnificent archway, under The Captain's Tower and crossed the triangular courtyard of the inner ward to the aforementioned St Mary's Tower. Entering the inner building we climbed two stories to the storage room where Robins had informed us that the regimental trophies and memorabilia were held. The soldier took a large key and opened the door. Inside was a veritable treasure trove; a stored wealth of valuables from all around the globe, won through two centuries of service by the Cumberland regiment.

It was to the door of the room however, that Holmes first turned his attention. In the rather gloomy light of the tower, Holmes took his small magnifying glass from his vest pocket. Striking a match, he held it up to the keyhole and peered into the small aperture through the lens. He went through several matches before he appeared happy with his observations and finally crossed the threshold of the room itself. The detective then glanced round focusing his attention on the one window. Moving towards it he gave it a cursory examination. Running his gloved fingers along the sill, studying the latch he gave a cursory 'Hmm' to himself. Almost as an afterthought Holmes then looked at some of the items within the room itself.

I have observed on many occasions that my friend pays little regard for the cleanliness of his clothes or the condition of any material items when he is on a case. Countless times, I have witnessed him wade fully clothed into water, crawl on hands and knees through mud or sift through the dust and ashes in an uncleaned fireplace, in an effort to find that vital clue. It was with little surprise therefore that I saw my friend climbing over boxes, throwing items away after studying them and generally treating the trophies of the regiment with disregard and contempt. I could not help being amused by

Robins's reaction to the detective's behaviour. Discomfort gradually turned to horror as he witnessed Holmes carelessly manhandle trophies and mementos from campaigns dating back some two hundred years and brought back from all four corners of the globe. The poor man was beside himself as he followed Holmes around the room, recovering discarded items, full in the knowledge that he would be held responsible for any damage.

[Queen Mary's Tower, Carlisle Castle]

"Were the colours and the drums of the French regiment stacked in any particular order?" Holmes questioned, as he tossed an elephant's tusk – elaborately decorated with silver bands – to one side.

"Not particularly sir," replied the junior NCO, scrambling to retrieve it.

After some minutes Holmes appeared to grow tired of his search and announced, "I have seen enough, we can leave now."

It was now twelve thirty and as we made our way back across the square Vaughan met us. "How is the investigation progressing?" he asked.

"It has been a most enlightening morning," replied Holmes.

"Excellent," said Vaughan, "I wonder if you would care to join me for lunch in the Officer's Mess?"

"That would be very pleasant," I said before Holmes could suggest otherwise.

Chapter Four

Several Interviews

We enjoyed a satisfying lunch of cold ham, creamed potatoes and salad in the mess. Holmes, as usual, ate little and as Vaughan and I retired to the lounge area for coffee and a cigar, Holmes said he needed to look around the castle and left us.

It was one thirty when Vaughan excused himself to carry on his duties and, as I knew that Holmes would be some time searching the medieval fortress from tower to dungeon, immersed in his own thoughts, I decided to take a walk around the perimeter.

Immediately adjacent to the castle I found a beautiful park which, given the pleasantness of the afternoon, provided the perfect setting for my after lunch stroll. The paths were lined with foliage – delightfully mixed colours of golden brown, copper and bronze – shed by trees that rustled gently in the early autumn breeze, and they led me to the centre of the park where I found myself gazing up at a magnificent statue of her late majesty. My reverie was broken by a voice from behind.

"Only put up last year." I turned to see an old man with an extraordinarily long white beard seated on one of the park benches behind me.

"Really?" I said politely. "It is a stunning likeness."

"Re-named the park in the great lady's honour," he added nodding.

My interest in the man increased when I noticed he was

wearing campaign medals on his jacket. He obviously saw me admiring them from afar, "Crimea and Indian Mutiny" he said proudly.

[Mr. Scott described the unveiling of the Queen's statue]

"India and Afghanistan" I countered, smiling. "Doctor John Watson" I continued, walking over to him and offering a hand.

"Isaac Scott" said the old man, gripping my hand with unusual strength for someone appearing so frail. "What regiment?" he asked, as I sat down.

"Northumberland Fusiliers and Berkshires."

"17th Lancers and local Yeomanry, myself."

"You weren't in the famous charge at Balaclava?" I asked in awe, knowing the former regiment named were involved in the infamous action.

"Alas no," he replied. "I joined them shortly afterwards. Saw plenty of action in India mind you," he continued. "That's where I picked up this damn injury". He reached down and rubbed the calf of his right leg grimacing as he did so.

"Yes," I said sympathetically, "I suffered myself at Maiwand," indicating my own war wounds.

"What brings you to our fair city?" asked the veteran.

"My friend and I are looking into a problem at the castle."

"Not the Arroyo Drums?" he questioned. Almost instantaneously, before I could answer, he cried, "Of course! Doctor Watson! Sherlock Holmes's Doctor Watson!"

I was both flattered by the recognition and astonished that he knew about the theft as I had assumed it was not public knowledge. Mr. Scott obviously saw my look of surprised and explained, "I work for Mr. Gibson, the tailor on Bank Street. We do a lot of work for the officers in the castle, so there's not much goes on that we don't know about. Found out about the scandal last Friday morning when I collected the uniforms used at last week's training at Penrith. I was tekin' 'em to be cleaned, you see. The story then broke in the paper on Friday night."

We continued to chat desultorily for some time, as old soldiers are bound to do, before I glanced at my watch. I was surprised to see that we had been sitting for almost two hours. I explained that I had an appointment at four o'clock and rose to leave, commenting that I was sure we would meet again before the investigation was completed.

"I hope so," the old man said genuinely, "goodbye for now." He walked away uncomfortably with the aid of a stick.

Given the hour and the time spent separated from Holmes I made my way back to the castle. As I walked in its shadow, created by the low, watery, late afternoon sun, I looked up and saw the unmistakable figure of my friend in his long travelling cape and matching ear flapped cap – appearing and disappearing behind the crenulated wall – as he prowled along the battlements, deep in thought.

He was descending as I walked under the portcullis into sight "Ah, Watson my boy! An interesting little problem," he said cryptically.

"What have you found?" I asked.

"Nothing," replied Holmes, amused by my puzzlement, "but that in itself may be progress".

"It is almost four o'clock," I said, "the Colonel will be waiting."

"That will never do," replied Holmes, further amused by my sense of urgency.

We rejoined Lt. Col. Hulme at the appointed hour and he informed us that the local police officer assigned to the investigation of the theft would be joining us shortly, "I have the feeling that once he heard about your involvement Mr. Holmes, interest and sense of importance in the matter has increased amongst the local constabulary. As Captain Vaughan stated earlier, Inspector Armstrong has a good reputation but I must say, some of his subordinates do not inspire confidence".

A few minutes later Lance Corporal Robins showed in a similarly youthful looking man. The latter had a most unusual gait; he did not so much walk, as lurch into the room, while his extreme leanness exaggerated his not inconsiderable height.

"Gentlemen," announced the Colonel, "let me introduce you to Sergeant Smith of the Cumberland Constabulary. Sergeant, these are the gentlemen I told you about on Monday."

"Pleased to meet you," said the man removing his hat. In doing so he highlighted his rather sallow complexion and revealed his head of dark, lank hair. "I took the liberty of wiring Inspector Lestrade who informed me that you have helped him on the odd occasion."

Helped on the odd occasion? I thought to myself. Holmes obviously read my mind and prevented me from speaking out with a glance and the merest of smiles, indicating that he intended to have some fun with our new acquaintance.

"Tell me Sergeant," said he, addressing the policeman, "what do you make of the case so far?"

"Case?" echoed Smith, "I don't think there is much of a case. As I said to my Inspector only the other day, it seems to be simply a matter of petty theft. I'm sure we'll have the musical instruments back in no time."

Out of the corner of my eye I saw the Lieutenant Colonel raise his eyes to the ceiling as he heard Smith's description of the regiment's prized trophies.

"Where do you think they are then?" asked Holmes simply.

"Well, er ..." stumbled Smith uncomfortably, "our resources are a little stretched at the moment. The truth is that we have yet to get our teeth into the case proper."

"What has been done then? The searching of the castle and its surrounding areas perhaps? Or the questioning of staff at the railway station about recent unusual freight?"

"Well er ... no, not yet, we were about to instigate such lines of enquiry," blustered the young policeman, unconvincingly.

"Well I am sure you will do your best Sergeant," said Holmes, with a mischievous twinkle, obviously sharing my amusement at the policeman's contradicting of himself, as to the importance of the case.

"We do have reason to believe that the theft is connected to the break in at the town hall," added the policeman, obviously trying to recover some credibility. By making this announcement, Smith did at least succeed in gaining Holmes's interest.

"When did this break-in occur?" asked the private consulting detective.

"Last Saturday night."

"And what was taken?"

"Strangely, very little. The only item missing was the plaque that lists the names of all past mayors of the city. It hangs – or hung – on the wall of the main chamber. It would appear that someone is playing silly beggars with our local history."

"If you have no objections sergeant, I would like to visit the scene of this burglary."

"Inspector Armstrong is in charge of both enquiries; I'm sure he would have no objection; I'll check with him when I get back. Mind you, our lads have given it a thorough going over. Unless you hear anything different I will tell them to expect you tomorrow morning. Well if you will all excuse me gentlemen, I have got quite a lot on at the moment," said Smith, as if to make a honourable withdrawal. Then as if to emphasise the importance of some of his tasks he added, "We are preparing for the visit of Sir Henry Campbell-Bannerman, the leader of the Liberal Party who is coming to the city on Friday. I shall return later in the week Colonel to update you on how *our* investigations are progressing."

His stressing of the word 'our' drew another half smile from my friend. Colonel Hulme did not share our amusement however. Upon the youthful sergeant's exit, he simply repeated his earlier phrase with a grave expression, "He does not inspire confidence."

"I wonder if we can speak with Private Nixon," said Holmes, re-capturing the Colonel's attention. "I would like him to accompany us to the hospital to see his colleague.

"He is on a charge at the moment. I am reluctant to allow him any privileges until further notice."

"Colonel Hulme, what's done is done and cannot be changed. Clearly this practice has been going for some time. Obviously I have no authority but I might suggest that you draw a line under the past and set the standards that your men should follow from now on. It is wrong to blame Nixon when some of his superiors clearly knew what was going on. I feel by allowing me to speak with Nixon and letting him accompany us to the hospital to see Walker, it will significantly help us get to the bottom of this matter." Holmes's tone was conciliatory and I had the impression that the commanding officer agreed, however reluctantly, with his suggestion.

"I will arrange for Nixon to be released to you," Hulme said, at last.

We left the commanding officer and went back to the room we had used earlier that day. Shortly afterward the charged soldier was brought to us. Holmes moved quickly to put him at his ease, "We are not the authorities Private Nixon; we are not here to apportion blame or to mete out sentences. We simply want to establish the facts of the case and solve the mystery surrounding the theft."

"I understand sir," replied the soldier quietly.

"Now, for what it is worth, how did you see the events of last Tuesday night?"

"Well sir, Jackie – that is Private Walker – and myself, took over sentry duties at twenty-two hundred hours. You probably know by now that I left my post shortly after."

"Exactly how long after," interrupted Holmes.

"It would be around twenty-two thirty hours sir. I then sneaked back into the barracks and left Walker to it, just as he had done with me the night before; it's common practice for us to alternate you see. It's just unlucky for Jackie that the trouble fell on his turn." There was genuine concern and guilt in the soldier's tone. "The following morning I went back to me post at 05.30 hours for the changing at 06.00. It was then that I found Private Walker. He was in a pretty bad state, having been lying there all night. I raised the alarm and got him some attention. He was moved up to the Infirmary shortly after and that's where the poor bloke's remained. I haven't seen him since coz I was arrested when the C.O. found out what had happened. I've been banged up since then."

"Did you suspect any theft at the time?"

"Well, to be honest sir, everything happened so fast. There was a lot of activity once I had raised the alarm but my only concern at the time was for Private Walker. It was only after that he had been taken to hospital that anything other than an attack by a bunch of drunkards occurred to me. I suggested to Major Young that it could have been otherwise. 'You are in enough trouble, without causing more, Private,' he said."

I glanced at Holmes; mindful of our meeting with the rather supercilious officer earlier that day, but his expression did not betray his thoughts. He simply informed the soldier, "I have spoken to Colonel Hulme and he has agreed to draw a line under the incident, given that it was a regular occurrence. He is more interested in the recovery of the drums than the punishment of his men."

"That's very kind of you sir, I'm sure the lads will appreciate it."

"Now I would like you to take us to the Infirmary to visit your colleague, I have cleared such a visit with Colonel Hulme."

"Certainly sir, I appreciate that. I'd like to see him myself, although they tell me he's still in a bad way."

"Perhaps you could show us exactly where you found Walker on the way," suggested Holmes.

The three of us walked across the square in the fading late afternoon light and Private Nixon pointed out to us the aforementioned toilet block. As we stood close to the single step he turned, pointed and said, "I came round the corner over there about half past five last Wednesday morning. It was still dark and as I came closer I saw a dark shape draped across this step. I thought at first it was an old coat but as I got closer I saw it was a man. It crossed my mind that an old tramp had sneaked in past Jack looking for shelter. But as I came to here" – he strode over to a particular point – "I saw the blood and the uniform; it was clear to me then that it was me mate."

"How exactly was Walker lying?" asked Holmes.

Nixon illustrated how his colleague was found by getting down on all fours and sprawling himself across the step, "He was lying" like this," he said, "with his legs inside the block and his upper body slouched outside."

"There must have been a considerable amount of blood," I ventured.

"Aye, there was Doctor. It was not only running down this gully to the drain down there, but there was quite a bit inside the block itself."

"That is most informative and quite suggestive," said Holmes. "Now could I propose that we make our way to see you colleague in hospital?"

We caught a tram opposite the castle for the half-mile or so, to the Cumberland Infirmary. Reporting to the reception area we were shown to the wing of the hospital where the injured soldier was. Private Nixon introduced us both and himself to a rather large, officious sister, who was obviously in charge of the ward. She informed us that Walker had shown some signed of improvement, as he had intermittently regained consciousness, during the past few hours. I asked her about his injuries and she explained that the skull had been fractured and an intracranial haematoma had been sustained in the attack.

"What's that?" asked Nixon.

"There was bleeding at the back of the head," I explained, indicating the area referred to at the rear of my own head.

"You can stay for a while gentlemen, but it is essential that the patient continues to rest," she said as she led us to his bedside.

A woman – obviously the patient's wife – was sitting by his bedside, clearly distressed by her husband's condition.

"Hello Rache," said Nixon, kissing the woman gently on the cheek, "how's he doing?"

"Still in a bit of a state," replied the sobbing Mrs. Walker.

"These gentlemen have come from London. They're trying to catch the buggers that did it."

After Nixon's introduction, Holmes spoke: "Forgive our intrusion madam, we will not stay long."

The sight of his friend and colleague, who was still bruised around the face and heavily bandaged, to protect the main wound at the back of the head, visibly shook Nixon. After a few minutes of standing over the patient, Walker appeared to be entering one of the semi-conscious periods the nurse had referred to earlier. He started to moan very lightly. Nixon started, and leaned forward. "Jackie, boy? It's Nico. How you feeling mate?" The crassness of his question almost immediately dawned on the soldier and this appeared to compound the discomfort he was already feeling through his pangs of guilt.

"Ask your friend if he could identify his attackers," Holmes said to Nixon.

"Jackie, can you remember anything about when you were bashed?" he said leaning close to Walker's ear. The latter continued to produce a barely audible moan. "He's trying to speak," said Nixon as he bent over still further until his ear was almost touching Walker's mouth.

"Can you make it out?" I asked, as I detected the injured man making a different sound.

Nixon screwed his face up as he strained still further to make out what was being attempted, "CH?" he said to himself, "Of course! Rache, he's calling for his wife Rachel. Don't worry mate," he continued, re-addressing his friend, "she's right here." He stood aside and allowed Mrs. Walker to lean over her husband.

"Jack?" she questioned. It seemed his drifting into semi-consciousness disturbed the poor woman even more.

"I must ask you to leave now gentlemen. You are tiring Mr. Walker out." We turned to find the sister approaching.

"Thank you for allowing our visit," said Holmes courteously. "Nixon, we must leave now."

The soldier took a longing look at his colleague and clasped his hand, "See you mate, I'll be back tomorrow." He kissed Mrs. Walker on the cheek once more, and we left to return to the castle, with our companion in an even more sombre mood than when we arrived, if that were possible. It was clear that his particular internal demons were having fun with their custodian at this time.

Upon our arrival at the regimental headquarters, we went our separate ways; Nixon returning to his barrack room, while Holmes and I strolled back along Castle Street to our lodgings after what I felt was a long and eventful day. As we walked, I told Holmes about my encounter in Victoria Park. He was most interested to learn of my conversation with old Mr. Scott and indicated that it may be worth paying him a visit.

"Surely the old man doesn't know anything about the robbery?" I asked.

"I would wager he has more information than even *he* realises," replied Holmes as we stepped from the street into the entrance of our hostelry.

[*The Crown and Mitre Inn – our accommodation in Carlisle*]

Chapter Five

A Mystery Solved

After a light breakfast the following morning, I accompanied Holmes to the town hall to inspect the scene of the burglary Sergeant Smith had referred to the previous afternoon.

The building itself was opposite our lodgings and as we climbed the dozen or so steps to the entrance, the elderly doorman afforded us a courteous welcome.

"Good morning gentleman, you will be the gentlemen from London. My name is Wilson. Inspector Armstrong notified us of your visit. Would you like some refreshment before you carry out you inspection?"

"Thank you, no" said Holmes. "I am only interested in the areas that were visited by the thieves."

I got the impression that poor old Wilson did not receive many visitors and he was quite excited about our interest in the break-in. I must say however that I appreciated his welcoming manner and my opinion of the local constabulary improved somewhat with the knowledge that the sergeant was as good as his word in informing his superior of our request, who in turn had obviously notified the local government office of our intended visit.

The doorman called over a colleague to take over his duties while he offered to show us the areas specified. He took us down into the basement area that had been the burglars' entry point. The soft putty and unpainted window frame was evidence enough of the repair work that followed their forced entry.

"They then forced the door to the stairs we have just descended," explained Wilson, "and went up to the council offices, again forced the door and unscrewed the plaque from the wall of the main chamber. I assume they then retraced their steps and left the way the entered."

[*We visited the Town Hall to inspect
the scene of the burglary*]

"Tell me," said Holmes, "has this theft been reported in the local press?"

"It was associated with the theft at the castle in Monday night's paper sir," replied Wilson.

"And this theft took place on Saturday night," Holmes added to himself. "That could be important. Tell me, where is the police station?"

"Left at the bottom of the steps sir and straight down Scotch Street."

"Thank you for your help Wilson; a very good morning to you."

As we descended the exterior steps of the building I sensed Holmes was troubled by what he had learned. "Perhaps we have been a little unfair on our official colleagues. It may well be that these two crimes *are* connected. Perhaps however, if they furnished us with all the evidence, we could make a balanced judgement. I think we should pay them a visit to discuss the matter further."

We followed the directions given by the doorman and found ourselves standing in front of the uniformed desk sergeant, in the reception area of the police station, within ten minutes.

[On our way to the police station, we passed the splendid market entrance on Scotch Street]

"Good morning, Sergeant, my name is Sherlock Holmes and this is my friend and colleague Doctor Watson. I wonder if you would be so good as to inform Inspector Armstrong that we wish to see him."

I could see by the poor man's face that he recognised our names but at the same time could not believe our presence; he peered at us as if we were characters from one of Monsieur Verne's science fiction novels. I took it from his reaction that our involvement in the case was not common knowledge around the police station. After a moment or two the sergeant stirred from his semi-trance and disappeared down a corridor. Some minutes later his colleague Smith, who we had met the previous afternoon appeared and showed us to an adjacent waiting room. "Inspector Armstrong will be with us shortly gentlemen," he said, and added, "he just had to nip out," without further elaboration.

Holmes sat in silence, with knitted brow, clearly troubled by something. I almost had the impression that he had underestimated the task at hand as his confident manner had all but left him. After waiting for a few minutes, a man of medium height with a large moustache entered the room.

"Good morning gentlemen," he said without any suggestion of superiority, "I am Cornelius Armstrong, I'm delighted to meet you. My apologies for having to send my sergeant to speak with you at the castle yesterday but I was otherwise engaged."

The policeman removed his coat and bowler hat. His piercing blue eyes shone out with the eagerness of a man half his age, and with the fervour of intense dedication to his chosen profession. Unlike our meeting with his colleague the previous day, I took an instant liking to the man.

"We appear to have a development," continued the policeman reaching in his pocket and producing a piece of paper. "This was left on the front desk anonymously this morning."

Holmes took the paper, read it and handed it to me. I read it out loud "'Call yourselves detectives? You lot couldn't catch a cold. Try the Cathedral later this week. See you then, or

60

maybe not!' The damned effrontery of them!" I said, as I handed the note back to the Inspector.

"What do you make of it, Mr. Holmes?" said the policeman who, unlike his subordinate, appeared to welcome my friend's help.

"It is difficult to say at this stage. I certainly did not anticipate this chain of events. One thing I do know Inspector is that we must work together, if we are going to solve these crimes." I was clear Holmes was referring to Sergeant Smith's attitude the day before.

"I assure you Mr. Holmes that if you and the Doctor consent to help solve these thefts, you will receive our full help and support."

As the Inspector was speaking there came great commotion from the front desk. I heard the desk sergeant shouting, "You can't bring that thing in here, we've just 'ad the floor cleaned!"

We all went out to see what the fuss was all about. In the middle of the front office stood a tall, well built man – a farmer apparently, judging by his dress. In his right hand, hung down by his side, he held a large wooden slab that almost reached the floor. The cause of the sergeant's consternation was the condition of the piece of timber. Not only was it dripping wet, it was also covered in a soggy moss and river weed, that was dripping on to the floor of the front office and consequently turning it green by the second.

"The lad found this in the beck on me farm," said the man, in an accent even broader than that of our host Mr. Graham. To the sergeant's further distress, he then lobbed the item of interest onto the desk, sending papers flying and splattering everything in a three-foot radius with sticky emerald slime. Holmes all of a sudden sprang forward and, without a thought for the appearance or the condition of his overcoat, swept the surface slime from the wooden plate with his forearm. As he did so, names and dates started to appear.

"Well I never," ejaculated Inspector Armstrong, as we looked on, "it's the Town Hall plaque!"

61

Holmes addressed the farmer. "You said your son found this Mr.?"

"Jennings. Yeah, that's right. Only this morning". I have a farm over the river in Etterby village"

"I would like to speak with the lad, if that is possible."

"Aye, he's in the cart outside, I'll just get him. BOY!" he hollered out of the main entrance door. A young lad of about eleven or twelve came running into the station. "Gentleman here wants to ask you about the plaque."

Although he appeared a rough and ready character, it is clear Jennings had raised the lad well, as he took off his cap in respect, as Holmes addressed him. "Is there anything you can tell me about this plaque, my young fellow?"

"No sir," said the lad. "I was tekkin' the dog out this morning and found it in the beck. I know it's a state but it was sitting near the top, so it can't have been there long."

"Did you see anyone in the area, who may have disposed of the plaque there?"

"No sir, though I saw a couple a strangers last night. milling about."

"You never said out!" interjected that lad's father.

Holmes waved away Jennings interruption. "What did they look like?" he asked the boy.

"Well, one was a big darkie, sir. I've never seen anybody that big before! His mate was much smaller, he "ad a bad arm an" leg."

"What?" questioned Holmes.

"Aye, he kept his arm close into his side and dragged his foot like this." The boy supported his narrative by acting the role of a cripple – hunched, and hobbling back and forth in the reception area of the police station.

At this Holmes appeared frozen to the spot. Everyone in the room stared at the consulting detective, before he himself broke the silence with an enormous roar of laughter. It took him some minutes to compose himself before he said, "My, my, they are a long way from home! Mind you I do applaud their sense of opportunism." With that he gave the boy a shilling and shook his father by the hand, thanking them both for their help.

As the two left, Armstrong said "Mr. Holmes I am at a loss to see what is so funny. And who, exactly are a long way from home?" I must confess I was pleased the Inspector asked this, as it was usually left to me to ask such questions, only to be left looking rather foolish by Holmes's answers.

"Well," started my friend, "I am pleased to say our investigations are back on track. But I am afraid gentlemen that you are in the presence of a complete imbecile. I have been as blind as a beetle." Seeing the collective puzzlement on the faces of the three policemen, and myself Holmes continued, "I do not believe the thefts at the castle and the town hall are connected gentlemen. I think opportunists committed the latter of these two break-ins as a smoke screen to their main aim. Perhaps I could explain fully over some refreshment?"

"But surely we should act quickly if we have made progress," I protested.

"Later, my dear fellow. There will be no further developments in either case for at least thirty six hours."

"Thirty six hours?" repeated Armstrong, "if something is going to happen over the next couple of days, I need to know about it Mr. Holmes, as it could compromise the visit of Sir Henry Campbell-Bannerman, the leader of the Liberal Party, who is visiting the city tomorrow. He will be arriving in early evening and giving a speech at the town hall, before returning to London on the sleeper. Security needs to be tight and I can ill afford to have men elsewhere on something that may or may not happen.

"If we take the necessary precautions, your dignitary's visit should not be affected. Perhaps I could explain fully in your office," suggested my friend.

Inspector Armstrong showed us to his office and instructed the sergeant to bring some coffee. Holmes, having shouldered out of his – by now almost ruined – overcoat, went to light a cigarette. "I do have some cigars, if you would prefer," said the Inspector.

"We are not home and dry yet," replied Holmes, "but why not a little self indulgence." We each took a cigar from the box offered by the policeman, just as the desk sergeant came in with a tray on which sat three mugs and a pot of appetisingly rich scented coffee. I took the liberty of pouring the liquid refreshment for all present and then addressed my friend.

"Holmes, I think I speak for both the Inspector and myself when I say that we are completely baffled by the events of the last hour" – Armstrong nodded his agreement – "and how are you so sure that the two thefts are unrelated, and *moreover*, that nothing further will happen until tomorrow night?"

"Saturday night, I'll wager," commented my friend. "You may recall Watson that when you brought the letter from Captain Vaughan to Baker Street on Monday last, I commented that this was the second time in as many months that the city of Carlisle had come to my attention."

"Vaguely," I assented.

"The first time the Border City was mentioned was by our old friend Inspector Gregson. He was in fact referring to a case I had the pleasure of assisting him with last year. A fairly straightforward case Watson, I had no need to impose on my trusty biographer. It involved a series of robberies with violence carried out by a particularly vicious gang. Although they started south of the river, they soon spread their wings over the whole of the capital, leaving a trail of destruction and injury before Gregson finally caught up with them as they attempted to break into the bank of Cox and Co. at Charing Cross."

I am sure Holmes delayed the final sentence of his narrative just long enough to allow me to take a mouthful of coffee. Upon hearing that it was my own bank that was the target of these brigands I coughed, spraying coffee into my lap, much to Holmes's amusement. Taking my handkerchief and wiping away the access from my trousers, I could not help but join in chuckling at Holmes's mischievous streak.

"The gang consisted of two brothers," resumed my friend, "Robert and his younger brother Raymond Adams, with the former prize-fighter Mike 'Boom Boom' Bennett and Alfie

Styles making up the numbers. It was the two latter gentlemen that young Jennings observed last night."

"Yes, of course!" I said, "I remember reading something of the case in the press, now you mention it, while I accompanied my wife on a trip to The Fens. But what on earth are they doing in this part of the world?"

"When Gregson received a tip-off that Cox and Co. was to be the subject of their next robbery, he asked me to inspect the interior with him. Upon inspecting the bank I observed a high skylight and deduced that this would be the gang's intended entry point. Gregson and I accompanied some of his officers on the night in question, inside the building ready to apprehend the gang as they broke in.

"Sure enough, the Adams brothers had devised a cunning plan that saw them not only enter through the skylight but lower themselves down into the bank via a large pulley system. Due to Styles's disabilities and Bennett's bulk it was the brothers themselves who utilised the giant pulley. It was only the two Adams' therefore who were picked up. Due to the ineptitude of the Scotland Yard force, they somehow neglected to capture their two associates who, it appears, escaped from the roof of the bank into the capital's grasslands.

"Consequentially, as it was only the brothers who were tried, convicted and sent to jail, Bennett and Styles set about breaking them out. Their first unsuccessful attempt was made some months ago and as a result, the Adams' were split up. Only last month Gregson informed me that the older brother was taken to York, whilst the younger Raymond was brought here to Carlisle – although I believe that his final destination is to be Durham."

Armstrong confirmed Holmes's final comment, "The local gaol is being utilised as an over-spill for Durham at the moment, as their jail is undergoing structural repairs and is receiving an upgrade in security," – then, musing to himself – "and the rest of this Adams Gang thought they could pull the wool and divert our attention in order to break out their man from our less secure County Gaol, before he went over the North East."

"You are quite correct, my dear Armstrong, and in reading of the theft of the Arroyo Drums in Friday evening's local newspaper gave them the perfect foot-hold. By adopting a policy of low risk but high profile burglaries, they stood every chance of deceiving the local force, fooling them into believing that there were to be a spate of such thefts. I would wager that the younger Adams will be moved within the next couple of days and his comrades will attempt to free him during his transportation."

"What do you suggest we do now?" asked the policeman.

"You have a perfect description of the two men we are looking for in connection with the town hall break-in; you should put all your available resource into ensure their swift arrest. Do not underestimate their capabilities however, Inspector. Styles's disabilities developed from his suffering from poliomyelitis as a child. That notwithstanding, he is as lithe as a cat and cunning too. His companion is a dangerous character – he is a veritable giant – and as you might imagine, has the strength to go with it. This man should be approached with great caution Inspector as he has, I'm afraid to report, been on the wrong end of too many refereeing decisions throughout his boxing career that have effected more than his confidence and ambition." Holmes tapped his temple with his forefinger to support this final comment.

"Watson and I will pay a visit to the governor of the County Gaol and inform him of our findings. In case your men do not pick up Bennett and Styles, I shall advise him to put extra guards on Adams."

"There is one other thing," I said as Holmes rose to leave. "We seem to have solved one mystery but what about the drums? Surely we are back to square one with that enquiry."

"Do not concern yourself for the moment, my dear fellow. I am confident that we will solve that mystery also within the next few days."

"I will telephone the governor to forewarn him of your visit," suggested Armstrong, "I will also send word to Colonel Hulme about this morning's events."

Holmes seemed reluctant to allow this at first, but eventually consented and we bade the Inspector good morning, setting off in the direction of the railway station to visit the governor of the County Gaol.

Chapter Six

Dr. Watson Is Uncomfortable

We walked the mile or so to the County Gaol that had been pointed out to us by Captain Vaughan shortly after our arrival in the city. We were met at the entrance to the imposing, dour looking building by one of the guards, who identified himself as Simmons, who informed us that the governor had been notified of our visit. He invited us to follow him to his governor's office.

As he led us along the endless maze of corridors and up several flights of metal stairs, our footsteps echoed around the hollow interior. One of his colleagues – acknowledging our approach – opened a metal gate that was barred to the ceiling and after we had walked through, he clanged it shut behind us. As he did so and turned the key, my heart skipped a beat. This fearful noise was repeated numerous times as we continued our journey and combined feelings of anxiety and claustrophobia threatened to engulf me. I was extremely relieved when we reached the governor's office after what must have only been a five-minute walk from the front entrance but somehow seemed longer.

Simmons knocked and entered. "Mr. Holmes and Doctor Watson from London, sir," – then turning back to us – "Gentlemen this is our governor, Mr. Lyons."

The large man rose from behind his desk and stretched out his hand. He bore a sallow complexion and his flaccid jowls were partly obscured by his thick side-whiskers. In all, his appearance and expression were in keeping with his place of work – grey and rather morose. I must stress that this was not a criticism of the poor man; I am sure I would look and feel exactly the same way if I were in his profession.

[*The entrance to the imposing, dour-looking County Gaol*]

"Good afternoon gentlemen," he said. "It is indeed a treat to have such distinguished visitors. I must confess to being puzzled however, as to the purpose of your visit. Although Inspector Armstrong notified me of your impending arrival, he did not elaborate as to the reason for it." Then, calling to his subordinate as the latter turned to leave, he asked, "Simmons, could you organise some tea please?"

"Very good sir," said the prison guard saluting.

"Now gentlemen," resumed the governor, as Simmons closed the door behind him, "how can I be of assistance?"

"You have a prisoner here, by the name of Adams?" said Holmes.

"Yes indeed, a most unsavoury character. Most of our inmates are local, petty criminals. Adams however is altogether a different kettle of fish, probably stemming from his London connection – no offence intended gentlemen. I will be pleased to see the back of him; he is being transferred to Durham at eight o"clock on Saturday night."

Holmes shot me a knowing glance. "You are quite accurate in your assessment of the individual in question Mr. Lyons. I must also advise you that he has two equally unsavoury associates – by the names of Styles and Bennett – who are in Carlisle as we speak and it is my hypothesis that an attempt will be made to break this ruffian out, possibly as he leaves the gaol or more likely, during transit on Saturday."

As Holmes introduced this revelation, the governor's jaw dropped and his thick bristling eyebrows – that had hitherto partially masked his lids – rose, as his large forehead creased with surprise. It was clear that, notwithstanding his unpleasant profession, he had never experienced such an exciting and unusual occurrence.

"What do you suggest we do Mr. Holmes?" he said as his complexion changed dramatically with excitement, bringing a more natural colour to his cheeks.

"I believe it would be wise to move young Adams sooner than previously arranged. Would I be correct in surmising that the journey was to be taken by road?" – Lyons nodded his response – "Then suggest you contact your colleagues in

Durham and advise them of a change in arrangements. I suggest you move him by rail tonight"

"I agree Mr. Holmes," said Lyons, quickly coming to terms with the disclosure. He continued, "what is more, I get very little pleasure in this job; so I think we should allow ourselves a little amusement. SIMMONS!"

It was as though the governor had psychic powers, as almost instantaneously the guard came in to the governor's office, not only responding to his cry but also carrying a tray of tea, in response to Mr. Lyons's earlier instruction.

"Have the prisoner Adams brought in would you, there's a good chap."

Holmes and I stared at each other, amused by Mr. Lyons's sense of sport.

We chatted idly for five minutes or so over our refreshment, before there was a knock on the door.

"ENTER!" cried the governor.

I sat at the right hand side of Mr. Lyons's desk, at a ninety-degree angle to the door. Holmes was sitting directly in front of the desk and as such could not be seen by anyone in the doorway.

Once Simmons opened the door, I turned in my chair to see him and the prisoner following. Although he was in my sight for only a second or two prior to his entrance into the office, I witnessed his contorted, almost arrogant expression that almost immediately led me to concur with Mr. Lyons's appraisal of the man. As he entered however and saw Holmes sitting there, the snarling look of contempt for his surroundings dropped to such an expression of incredulity I had never before witnessed. It was clear that my friend was the last person he expected to see.

"*What ... the ...?!*" was all the criminal could utter as he stared in disbelief.

"Good afternoon Adams," said Holmes coolly, "how are you enjoying this northern air?" He sounded like a vicar in a drawing room, he was so mild, and it was clear his meaningless question did not register with the villain, as the expression of amazement on the face of the latter did not alter.

72

"We are wise to your intentions Adams," – it was the governor's turn to have his fun – "Mr. Holmes has advised us of your associates" presence and your planned escape. Well let me tell you, my man, I have never had a prisoner escape when under my authority, and I have no intention of allowing *you* to blemish that record. Your transference to Durham will be brought forward and with a little good fortune, the authorities will arrest your colleagues before they can create further disturbance. Take him away!"

Simmons led Adams away, his demeanour – with slumped shoulders and sombre face – in marked contrast to the brash, self assured individual that entered the office some moments earlier.

After he left, the governor addressed my companion once more, "Mr. Holmes I cannot thank you enough. I will arrange for the prisoner to be sent across to Durham tonight."

"Very prudent," agreed the detective. "There is one more thing however. No doubt some of your staff frequent the public house outside?"

"Indeed they do, more's the pity. Its nickname is well merited, as it is a constant tap into the affairs of the gaol. It is a permanent source of concern to me; any little snippets of information that are overheard, are invariably embroidered and usually ending up causing problems either inside the gaol itself or in the local press."

"Well perhaps on this occasion we can turn this tittle-tattle to our advantage. I don't doubt that Styles will be a regular in the Inn during his visit because of its close proximity to the prison, and any slip of the tongue regarding Adams will, I'm sure, flush him and Bennett out of their hiding place. When they do appear, I will ensure that Inspector Armstrong and his colleagues will be there to apprehend them. To help Armstrong still further, bearing in mind he is nervous about his dignitary's visit tomorrow and his shortage of men, perhaps we could arrange our little scheme for Saturday night, around six o'clock?"

"I'm sure that can be arranged Mr. Holmes," replied Lyons, "I will arrange to have Simmons and one of his colleagues in the pub at the appropriate hour."

"Excellent! I would wager that the conspicuous Styles would be in there, in preparation for the attempted breakout later that evening. If I am correct in my hypothesis, his colleague will join him at the appointed hour. When Styles hears of your prompt action in removing their colleague, he will move to prevent Bennett showing up and look to arrange their transport out of the city."

With that, Simmons returned to escort us from the building and – with the governor's permission – Holmes explained the plan to the guard, pointing out the unusual appearance of Styles due to his disability. "Do not divulge the information concerning Adams until you are happy that Styles is present," said my friend to the prison warden.

Once out on the street again, the air somehow tasted fresher. I was surprised by my own reaction to being in the gaol – having experienced most things in this life – but I was overwhelmed by a tremendous feeling of incarceration. It was now late afternoon and we made our way back to the Crown and Mitre.

"Ah, Mr. Holmes," said Graham as we entered, "a note was left for you earlier". He reached down behind a makeshift counter and produced a grubby looking brown envelope.

"Who left it?" asked my friend.

"I dunno sir, it was here lyin' when I cem up from the cellar earlier."

"Thank you," replied Holmes, taking the envelope. Far from administering his usual thorough examination of such an item, he ripped it open and looked briefly at the single sheet of paper contained within. "Hmm, an interesting development," he said handing the paper to me.

"In connection with the primary case, I hope," I said.

"Indeed."

I looked at the paper and found only two words written: 'SINN FIENE'. I must confess to being completely bemused by the message. "What does it mean?" I asked.

"It is Irish; literally translated it means 'Ourselves Alone'". Then ignoring my bewilderment Holmes called out "Billy?"

The young chap who had carried our bags up to our room the previous day suddenly appeared. As an aside, it has been my experience that Holmes had a habit of calling all young lads of that age "Billy", whether that is there given name or not. That said, the youngster answered Holmes's call and came over ready to assist.

"Tell me young fellow," started Holmes, "where is the Irish quarter in Carlisle?"

"You wanna go down Caudigate to Blue Lugs 'n the Sailor sir," said the boy.

Holmes and I stared at each other, barely comprehending a word the lad had said. Seeing our confusion Billy said, in a mock Queen's English accent "Perhaps you gentlemen would like to head in the direction of the Cumberland Infirmary and visit the Caldewgate area of town, immediately to the west of the castle and frequent the Joiner's Arms Inn and Jovial Sailor Tavern." With that, the little scallywag waltzed off with his nose in the air.

"What shall we do now?" I asked

"There's only one thing for it Watson," said Holmes with apparent seriousness, forcing me to hang on to his every word, "it's off to Blue Lugs!" Struck by the absurdity of the young lad's dialect and the nickname given to the former of the two pubs, we simultaneously burst into a roar of laughter.

After recovering our composure, we retraced our steps back towards the castle and followed the young lad's westerly directions, remembering our own journey to the Infirmary the previous day to visit the injured Walker. Travelling on the tram I did not take much notice of the route but now I saw that the area mentioned was a wide street that was self-contained within a natural bowl. It was clear from the architecture and condition of the surrounding streets that this was an impoverished area and when we found the aforementioned 'Joiner's Arms', I thought to myself how reluctant I would have been to enter such an establishment on my own. Holmes however, did not hesitate and purposefully strode into the pub.

As we entered I was instantly struck by the commingled – almost overpowering – stench of stale beer, rank tobacco smoke and perspiration. My suspicions regarding the clientele were instantly confirmed; the tavern was full of what could best be described as a gang of ruffians. The collection of evil and violent looking characters were a veritable rogues' gallery as they all appeared to sport either a cauliflower ear or a broken nose, or both. They were certainly individuals one would not like to meet on a dark night and to a man they all looked up as we walked entered their den.

The pub itself was basic in the extreme with stone floors and trestle tables. Upon approaching the landlord, the ridiculous nickname given to his establishment became apparent. Not only was he a barrel-chested, dirty, unshaven individual, but also his oversized ears were a distinct shade of indigo! His nose was also threatening to follow suit and it was my professional opinion that this was a clear result of him drinking most of his profits.

Sadly, his manner did not compensate for his appearance. "What can I get ye?" he grunted at us.

"Two pints of your finest ale landlord," said Holmes without prejudice.

The man filled two tankards and slapped them onto the bar, spilling a proportion of the contents as he did so. I peered down in the rather murky, non-too appetising liquid. Holmes on the other hand grabbed his tankard with great enthusiasm and made for the table seating the roughest looking characters in the establishment; an honour for which, it must be said, there was strong competition.

In spite of our uncomfortable surroundings it has been my experience, on more than one occasion, to witness Holmes immediately defuse a potentially dangerous situation by sitting down with the locals and without any inhibitions speaking to them on a level and on subjects they can instantly relate to.

"May we join you gentlemen? It is nice to have some liquid refreshment after a hard day's work."

There was a collective snigger before a spokesman for the table said "Ye don't look as though ye've done much plate layin' today!"

Sniggers turned to laughter, which Holmes joined in heartily. "That is perfectly true," said he. "I travel on the railway frequently but seldom lay the tracks!"

This brought even more laughter from the table and the men, obviously impressed and amused by Holmes's self-derogatory remark, made room at the table for their visitors. As their appearance suggested, the group were all either railway navvies or labourers. Holmes quickly won their trust and within a few minutes he was laughing and joking with the whole group as if he had been acquainted with them for years. Holmes demonstrated once more that he is equally at home conversing with paupers or princes, and I decided after observing him for a short while, that my admiration for my friend knew no bounds.

After thirty or forty minutes Holmes announced – while flashing me a glance to meet him at the bar – "I must leave you now, gentlemen. But allow me to get in a round before I go."

"Hey-hey!" sang one, instantaneously.

"A true gent!" added another, while the rest chorused their approval.

"It is clear they cannot help us," Holmes said to me as we walked over towards the bar, "I wonder if we will have more luck with the landlord. Then addressing the publican he continued, "I would be obliged if you provided my friends with a further beverage and "– *sotto voce* – "provide me with some information."

The man's mouth contorted into a threatening snarl until his greedy eyes spotted the gold sovereign Holmes held on the bar under the index finger of his right hand. The snarl turned to an avaricious smile that revealed two yellow, rotting teeth protruding from the middle of his lower gum – their siblings were all missing.

"What sort of information?" he asked, not taking his eyes from the coin.

"I need to know if there have been any strangers in the area over the past few days".

"Strangers?"

"I noticed your miniature Union Flag position behind the bar, suggesting that you are on the Unionist side of the sectarian divide. That notwithstanding I would wager that there are no visitors to this area of town – regardless of politics or religion – that would go unnoticed by your good self."

"You mean have there been any bloody Fenians?"

"Precisely."

"Well, there were some strangers in 'ere a-couple-a-weeks ago but I couldn't say who they were. Never seen 'em since" His eyes never left the sovereign for a moment.

"How many?"

"Four or five. They sat quietly over there," he said jerking his head in the direction of a secluded corner.

"How did they behave?"

"As I say, very quiet. There was only one did any talkin'. Another bloke joined them after a while. I noticed again that the new bloke spoke only with the leader. The others just sat there like idiots."

"Thank you landlord," said Holmes, releasing the coin, "you have been extremely helpful." We turned to leave but as we reached the door, my friend said "Oh, Watson, there is something I forgot. I'll be back in an instant." He turned back leaving me at the door, to re-address the barman. I could not hear what was said above the din, but the supplementary interview only lasted a few seconds and I saw the landlord nodding his greasy head. Holmes then turned again to join me in our exit and shouted to his drinking companions, "And a very good evening to you gentlemen!" They cheered their response and raised their newly filled tankards.

When we were outside Holmes said, "An interesting episode; the dear old publican rarely overlooks a new customer."

"It is a pity he is not as enthusiastic about his personal hygiene!" I replied, much to Holmes's amusement. "On to the Jovial Sailor Tavern then?"

"No," said my friend, "we will find nothing more there. Regardless of the sectarian divide amongst the local population, as I suggested to the landlord, visitors to the area would be known to everyone. No, we should make our way back Watson and think about what we have learned today."

I must confess to being a little relieved at being spared a similarly uncomfortable half-hour in what would be no doubt equally threatening surroundings. I pulled my collar up still further to combat the distinctly chill wind that grabbed at our coats, and accompanied Holmes back to our lodgings.

After the excitement and exertions of the day I had a hearty appetite and enthusiastically tucked into a rather substantial steak and kidney pudding, laid on for us by our hostess Mrs. Graham. For his part Holmes ate little, preferring to mull over the occasional cigarette and stare idly into space.

"There's something missing," he said absentmindedly.

"Of course there is – the Arroyo Drums." I said, amused by my own sharpness. Holmes did not so much ignore my facetiousness; my comment simply did not register in that magnificent brain as it explored every detail of the case at hand.

"I think we need to speak with the chap I would wager is the most trustworthy character in the regiment," he said, again half to himself.

"Vaughan?" I questioned.

"No, no," he said sharply, snapping out of his mental case analysis, "Sergeant Armstrong of course!"

With that he rose from the table bidding me goodnight, leaving me to try and fathom the mystery.

Chapter Seven

An Interview With Sergeant Armstrong

The following morning we set out once more on the short journey to the castle and found that it had been raining through the night, although there was a certain amount of humidity in the air. As we walked, I commented once more to my friend how changeable the weather was in this northern English county.

"That said," I added, "I must say I prefer this altogether fresher climate to the rather dense atmosphere of the capital."

Upon our arrival, we were shown to the Sergeants' Office where, shortly thereafter, Sergeant George Armstrong met us, after being informed of our request to speak with him.

"Morning Gentlemen," he said as he entered.

"Good morning Sergeant," I said, "a change in the weather this morning."

"Yes, there is a storm brewing I think," replied the local man.

"I'm sorry we missed you the other day Sergeant, I believe you were unavailable," said Holmes.

"That's right sir, Captain Vaughan asked me to go through to Penrith and review last week's exercise with the Commanding Officer of the local Yeomanry regiment."

"Is that a standard practice?"

"Yes sir, although one of the officers normally holds the review session. Lord Lonsdale – the 5th Earl – is the Commanding Officer; his family have run the Yeomanry regiment since his grandfather raised the troop back in 1819. When he assumed command in 1897, he introduced such reviews. Annual training for the part time boys was increased from ten days to eighteen days a couple of years ago and I think the Earl likes to keep his lads as efficient as possible, so he uses part of the annual training session as a useful examination by his full time colleagues. After the weeks training is complete, he views any feedback as invaluable.

"I suppose with all the carry on surrounding the drums, it was easier to send me back to Penrith on this occasion," concluded the sergeant.

"Quite probably," mused Holmes. "Tell me Sergeant Armstrong, how many uniforms did you use last week?"

"The officers and NCO's each use two sir; as I say, it is not only a ceremonial inspection of the part-timers but an active training session, where we perform various exercises with them."

"And how is the relationship between the part timers and their regular colleagues?"

"They're good lads in the main – it's an enjoyable week. Some of the lads were with us during the Boer War, which was the Yeomanry's first overseas campaign."

"Did anything unusual occur while you were in Penrith?"

"Well as I said earlier sir," – Armstrong smiled to himself – "I reckon they'll be a storm before the weekend is out, but it can't possibly be as bad as the one we had a week gone Tuesday night."

"The night of the theft?" interrupted Holmes, "Nixon never mentioned anything about a storm when I questioned him." He sounded a little piqued by the private soldier's omission.

"Well he's got enough on his plate without worrying about the weather," quipped the Non Commission Officer, "but I can assure you that last Tuesday night it put down enough water to refill the canal!"

"Canal?" questioned Holmes.

"Well it's a railway now," resumed Armstrong. "Originally built to link the city with Port Carlisle. The city is a big

82

industrial centre you see, and it needs an outlet to the Solway basin. Now the railway line runs down to Silloth Docks."

I thought I saw a suggestion of a smile pluck at Holmes's lips. Rather than pursue the merits of the weather and local communication links however, the detective invited Sergeant Armstrong to return to the subject at hand.

"It was ironic really," resumed the soldier, "because we were out under canvass and I was chatting with some of the lads about the battle at Arroyo when the boys captured the drums in the first place. The night before the battle was just like that, you see. There was I trying to convince the lads that we had it good compared to our erstwhile colleagues who had to fight in such conditions, and all the while, our drums were being stolen.

"As you might imagine, the following morning the field was virtually waterlogged. We were due to perform an exercise that simulated a cavalry advance with infantry support. Conditions were treacherous for man and beast alike. When the exercise started, more than one horse unseated its rider, probably through a combination of conditions underfoot and the soaking wet equipment."

"Was there any suggestion of equipment being tampered with?"

"No sir," said Armstrong, surprised by the apparently irrelevant question. He continued his narrative. "One by one, columns proceeded across the field with a member of the regulars leading the infantry support. I remember one casualty in particular, Major Dalston-Ewbankes, of the Yeomanry force, a chap from out Appleby way. He fell and was quite badly injured. Captain Vaughan, who was in charge of his particular support force had to organise his removal from the field. We were all amused to see Harry blustering away, clearly miffed that his squadron had disrupted the exercise. I think he'd had enough as, with the help of a couple of part-timers he personally took the old boy off to the local hospital. By the time he got back the exercise was all but over. He received a bit more ribbing from the lads about that."

The Non Commissioned Officer then corrected himself, "Hang on a minute, I've got that wrong! You asked me about the uniforms? I forgot that after the exercise we contacted Gibson, our tailor and organised old Isaac to come and collect the kit we had used that day. The C.O. felt it unnecessary to have the dirty uniforms clogging up the camp. The old boy had the foresight to bring replacements with him."

"Is that the chap with the long white beard?" I asked and – responding to Armstrong's nodded reply – added "I met him in the local park earlier this week. I believe he used to be in the Yeomanry himself?"

"Yes, that's right. He also belongs out Penrith way, so when he came out on the Wednesday with his experiences and local connections, we could hardly get rid of him! He's a grand old bloke mind you; I've got a lot of time for him. Seen a bit of action himself in his time too," said the regular, obviously referring to the old man's time spent in India and the Crimea.

"And the rest of the week?" asked Holmes, obviously keen to pull Armstrong back to the subject at hand.

"The rest of the week passed off without further incident as I recall."

"Since your return, have you found any anomalies concerning the men's uniforms?"

"How did you know that sir?" said the sergeant, amazed by Holmes's question. "There was an incident only yesterday. I was carrying out a routine inspection in the barracks, when I found two dirty uniforms belonging to a couple of the boys that were with us in Penrith. After giving them a good rollicking," he added, with a smile, "I just put it down to their mates playing a prank on them. I didn't really think it was too important sir," he concluded.

"There is nothing more important than trifles Sergeant," said Holmes smiling.

I thought Armstrong prevaricated rather with his answers and embroidered them unnecessarily but I suppose that is the prerogative of all veteran soldiers, perhaps even myself if I'm perfectly honest. That notwithstanding, there was no suggestion from him of any superiority over his subordinates or his part time colleagues and I must say, I was impressed by this obviously honourable and hard working soldier. I sensed that Holmes shared my view.

"I understand you have a loyalty to your regimental colleagues," then said the detective, "but how do you rate your officers?"

Only a non-military man could ask such an indiscreet question and I could see that Armstrong was uncomfortable with this line of questioning.

"Come, come, Sergeant," prompted Holmes, "there are only the three of us here, and you can count on our complete integrity and discretion".

"Well to be honest with you sir," answered the soldier, in a lowered, yet reassured tone, "I don't know many of the officers very well, never having worked closely with them. The only two I feel comfortable with are the C.O. himself and 'H', er – Captain Vaughan that is – I served with them both in South Africa – good blokes the pair of them – well thought of by the men. We all felt Harry was unlucky to be pipped for the Major's position earlier this year."

"Yes, I think we met the successful candidate earlier this week, Major Young?"

"That's right sir, he came from nowhere to get the job. He was with the 2nd Battalion who have been in Burma all year. We didn't know much about him to till he took up post." Although Armstrong did not elaborate on his opinions of Young, I sensed that he did not rate him as a superior officer. Instead he continued describing his friend and colleague from South Africa, "I've been on many an operation with 'H'; had to reign him back on a couple of occasions; always the first man out of the traps, all guns blazing," he said.

"Yes I can testify to that," said I, about to recount my experience of our retreat to Kandahar

"Thank you Watson," interrupted Holmes sharply, inviting Armstrong to continue.

"The truth is sir that the regiment is still finding its feet after the Boer War. Lost a lot of blokes over there, many others left on our return and a few new officers have joined from other regiments".

"Yes, speaking of those who have transferred; what do you make of the new Regimental Sergeant Major?"

"Seems strangely quiet for somebody so senior. I spoke with him in the mess during his first week – it's usually good to form the bond in the social environment," he added smiling at me, aware of my knowledge of such military matters. "He was a bit off hand to be honest. I was just making general conversation. He said his parents moved to Newcastle from Ireland back in the mid fifties. Joined as a boy soldier apparently and worked his way up through the Northumberland regiment before getting the Regimental Sergeant Major role with us.

"'What action did you see with the Fusiliers?' I asked.

"'Enough,' was his curt reply.

""Knowing the Northumberland Fusiliers were themselves on the sub continent some years back," – Armstrong nodded at me to confirm his awareness of my brief military adventure with the regiment – I asked 'Were you with the regiment in Indian and Afghanistan?'

"'Not that it's any of your business,' said the RSM, 'no, I was not,' and then made it clear that he was not going answer any more questions from the likes of you."

I had cast a glance toward Holmes at Armstrong's mention of Ireland but his face did not betray his thoughts. It is surely unthinkable that such a responsible figure as the RSM – regardless of his reticence and strange behaviour – could somehow be involved in such a crime, I thought to myself.

"There were a few rumours among the lads that it was a bit of a diplomatic move for him when he left the Fusiliers. It's said that he wasn't a particularly well-liked figure in Newcastle. Then there was some other nonsense about him changing his name."

"And what is your view of these rumours, Sergeant, do you feel they have any foundation?"

*[The case was the subject of much discussion amongst the
soldiers of the Border Regiment]*

"I don't like rumours myself, despite his appearance and
behaviour, I believe in giving the bloke a chance. Besides he –
like the rest of us – is here to do a job, not to make friends."

"Quite correct, and commendable Sergeant Armstrong,"
complimented Holmes. "Finally, where is the nearest Post

Office?" Both Armstrong and I were taken aback by the apparently unrelated question.

"As you leave the castle sir, at the bottom of the moat-bridge, turn left and cross the road; you'll find one a couple a hundred yards down the street on your right hand side."

"You have been most helpful Sergeant, thank you," said Holmes.

"Not at all," replied the soldier, appearing not to be aware of his helpfulness – a feeling I must confess to sharing.

As we rose to leave I said to the soldier, "Captain Vaughan told us that you and the Inspector are cousins, Sergeant?"

"Yes, that's right sir, more like brothers if truth be told. We grew up together both wanting to join the army. Our interest came from Corny's dad who was with the local regiment himself. It's funny that you mentioned old Isaac, as you did before, because as I always think of Corny's dad when I see him. Isaac served with Sir Evelyn Wood in the Mutiny, you see. It was to Wood's ill-fated regiment that Uncle John later transferred into. The whole family was devastated when he was killed in 2nd Ashinti War in West Africa in the mid seventies; we were just kids at the time. Army barmy we were, from reading history books to the two of us simulating the Battle of Waterloo in grandma's front parlour. As we grew up, Corny - being an only one - felt obliged to stay and look after his mam. She was dead against him joining anyway, having lost Uncle John, so he ended up joining the local force. That way he could see some service while staying in the city. Meanwhile I managed to fulfil our childhood ambition. We both started our respective careers in the mid eighties and, I suppose we've not done bad for ourselves."

Corny and Geordie, I thought to myself – I thought the two of them sounded like a vaudevillian comedy duet! I must say however, that I had taken a liking to both men.

Although he would never admit to it, I suspected Holmes shared my view. We turned to leave and he said, "Thank you once again for you help Sergeant."

As we left the Sergeants" Office, Lance Corporal Robins met us, and he informed us that Lt. Col. Hulme requested an update on the case. We entered the Colonel's office to find the Commanding Officer standing behind his desk, with his hands behind his back, looking out onto the square.

"Gentlemen," he said as we entered, "forgive my impatience but I am eager to know how the investigation is progressing."

"I am still gathering data," said Holmes, "but I feel we are making progress."

"Do you think we can recover the drums Mr. Holmes?"

"I am confident that we can identify the perpetrators of the crime Colonel, but I am afraid we will have to rely on good fortune if we are to recover your prized drums."

"Perpetrators?" repeated the Commanding Officer, "you think more than one man is behind this?"

"Undoubtedly, there has been much planning gone into this operation. The evidence I have at the moment points to the involvement of five people. Do not give up hope however, Colonel, I suggest you continue to prepare for Arroyo Day."

Ignoring Holmes's revelation about the number of gang members, Hulme instead addressed my friend's latter comment. "What is the point of preparing for the day without the drums? They are the whole point *of* the day. We will be a laughing stock if we do not have them." The colonel made no attempt to hide his frustration.

"I believe it would help the case if we continued as if nothing were amiss," Holmes continued in his attempt to assuage the colonel, "I assure you that in the meantime my friend and I shall make every effort to make the day complete."

"I can ask no more," said the Commanding Officer, still a little crestfallen. "This is a sorry business, gentlemen. Not only the theft but the highlighting of our lax security is causing me great embarrassment."

"I would suggest, Colonel Hulme, that you have been in greater positions of threat and danger than this throughout you career," said my friend, "do not torture yourself unnecessarily."

"You are quite correct Mr. Holmes but that is exactly the problem. I have experienced much to be proud of in my career but that will all count for nought if we do not recover the Arroyo Drums. I must take full responsibility of the actions all the whole regiment and as such, I will always be remembered as the Commanding Officer that ran a far from tight depot, and who's security lapses culminated in the regiment losing its most prized trophy."

"I repeat that the case is not over yet, Colonel, and my friend will confirm that I am rarely defeated, when faced with the various problems that come my way."

"I hope you continue your success," said the senior soldier.

"Before I complete my investigations however, I must broach a delicate subject with you." After a suitable pause, to allow his comments to sink in, the detective continued, "could you tell me your views on Major Young and RSM McCue?"

The commanding officer had to visibly keep a tight hold of his composure before answering with a slightly higher tone, "To compound my problems, are you telling me that you have suspicions about my own men?"

"I am keeping an open mind at this stage," replied Holmes, matching the colonel's tone, "but it is important to rule nothing out at this stage."

Succeeding in keeping his emotions in check, Colonel Hulme addressed Holmes's original question, "Both men have not been with us that long. Major Young was *with* the Regiment but was out in Burma with the 2nd Battalion. I heard good reports from his Commanding Officer and he had a good interview. Beyond that I do not think there is a great deal to report, it has been a fairly quiet year for the home battalion and he has not had the chance of showing us what he can do. Having said that the first opportunity he gets of commanding the depot and the damn drums go missing! Hardly an auspicious start, now I think about."

"And McCue?" prompted Holmes.

"Well, we know even less about him, as he has been with us less than a month. I must say I find him a little morose for someone in the position of dealing with all ranks but again, he came with glowing references and I have seen nothing so far that suggests he is anything other than a fine soldier."

"Thank you Colonel, I shall keep you informed of our progress."

With that we left the Lieutenant Colonel to ponder the situation.

"Now Watson," said Holmes, as we walked across the square, "I need to send off my telegram and then I think we should pay Inspector Armstrong a visit to discuss our intentions for Saturday evening."

So engrossed was I in the events of the day and the various clues uncovered by Holmes, I had completely forgotten about the preliminary plan my friend had devised to snare the London criminals. I followed my friend down the cobbled pathway that crossed the exterior moat, onto the street outside, with both cases wrestling for attention in my head.

Chapter Eight

A Newspaper Story

It was early afternoon by the time we left the castle and followed Sergeant Armstrong's directions towards the Post Office, where Holmes sent his telegram – 'To London' – he said without elaborating.

"And now to pay the Inspector a visit to discuss the details of tomorrow's apprehension of Styles and Bennett," he added, as he rejoined me on the street outside.

"That is unless his men have captured them already," I said.

My companion did not respond verbally to this view but simply gave me a look of surprise, which seemed to suggest that he felt that possibility was highly unlikely. We continued our journey in silence.

We found a hive of activity upon our arrival at the police station. The same desk sergeant was on duty as the previous day and he greeted us cordially, "Good afternoon gentlemen, you'll have to excuse the mayhem, we are getting ready to receive our VIP tonight."

"I understand," said Holmes, "could you inform Inspector Armstrong we would like to speak with him?"

"I'll see if he's available."

In a repeat of the previous day's scene, we waited some minutes for the Inspector to see us. The sergeant then showed us into his office, where we found him on the telephone, obviously to a colleague.

"Yes I am aware of that fact. Nevertheless, the leader of Her Majesty's Opposition will be arriving tonight and we have to at least *appear* as though we are prepared!

"Good afternoon Mr. Holmes, Doctor," said the policeman, as he replaced the earpiece on the cradle of the candlestick telephone. "I am afraid I cannot spare you much time."

"I understand fully Inspector, but I must inform you of our visit to the prison to see Adams," replied Holmes.

He proceeded to recall the events that took place after we left the police station the previous day. He concluded by informing Armstrong of his plan to snare the two London gang members once they were aware of their colleague's early transfer.

"If you have some of your men available from six o'clock onwards, we will see if we cannot succeed where your Scotland Yard colleagues failed," said Holmes.

"I appreciate your efforts Mr. Holmes; I shall be waiting here at six for your instruction. I wonder if I could impose on you further however? As you know Sir Henry Campbell-Bannerman is visiting tonight and I am concerned about disruption of any sort. Would you be so kind as to make *yourselves* available, just in case Styles, Bennett – or anyone else for that matter – decide to cause some kind of disorder."

"Certainly Armstrong," said my friend without hesitation, "unless I have an early reply to my telegram, I do not think we will have anything else to occupy our time."

It was clear to me that Holmes was warming to the professional detective. It has been my experience that when Holmes sees someone in direct opposition, he has no time for them, but if they show a willingness to work alongside, he will make every effort to support the cause, even to the point of allowing the official forces to take full credit for solving the mystery they were jointly involved in; something that I have consistently disagreed with, but something that Holmes has consistently allowed to happen.

"If you could be at the railway station for seven then," said the policeman.

"We will see you then."

We made our way back to our lodgings, where my companion grew increasingly agitated. He prowled around the sitting room like a caged animal, much to my annoyance as I was trying to read that morning's newspaper. I finally suggested that we take an afternoon stroll.

"Perhaps you are right," said Holmes.

We donned our hats and coats once more and left the Inn, walking with nowhere in mind but in a southerly direction. Holmes was in a world of his own, walking with his chin on his chest relying on me for direction. Although my companion was no company whatsoever, when he was in this kind of mood, I must say I preferred to be outside and was therefore please that I had coaxed him out of our cramped quarters.

It struck me once more during our promenade how changeable the temperature was in this part of the world; only twenty-four hours earlier it had been bitterly cold and now it was really quite warm. My mind wandered back to Holmes's interview with Sergeant Armstrong who had predicted a thunderstorm within the next few days.

We had walked in silence for over an hour when we found ourselves once more at the southern end of the bustling English Street, heading back to the Crown and Mitre. Suddenly as we passed one of the adjoining streets Holmes casually announced, "I shall see you back at the Inn in one hour Watson," and with that – much to my bewilderment – he made an abrupt right turn and made off as if he knew exactly where he was going.

As I stood looking at my friend in surprise, as he walked away, my daydreaming was interrupted by the newspaper vendor, standing at the right-angled junction of the two streets just described, "*EARLY EVENING EDITION! CLERGYMAN AND SCHOOLMISTRESS SCANDAL!*" he cried in that distinctive lilt, apparently common to all of those in his profession, "*NOT MANY LEFT!*"

I walked over the few paces and bought one of his papers, amused to see that the 'not many left' consisted of over a hundred copies stacked behind his barrow.

[English Street, Carlisle]

"Thank you sir," he said as I handed over a shilling. Turning, I chuckled at his follow up holler; *"THERE'S NO MORE AFTER THIS!"*

The headline and lead story raised a smile. It related a flowery tale of a married vicar in one of the more isolated parts of the county who had been discovered having an indiscreet relationship with the unmarried local schoolmistress! Upon discovering this atrocity – committed by two of the supposed upstanding members of the community – a gang of local men – acting as vigilantes – had taken an ancient form of retribution against the clergyman by tying him to a gate and humiliating him still further, by parading him through the streets of the village. The story concluded by stating that the schoolmistress had disappeared after the local police had made several arrests. The matter was being referred to the Kirkby Stephen magistrates.

I thought to myself how simplistic life must be in the provinces, as they do not experience the crime we regularly suffer in the capital. My thoughts then drifted to Inspector Armstrong and how different his job must be from his colleagues from Scotland Yard. Like Holmes, I myself was warming to Armstrong who – unlike so many of his official colleagues, who appeared at first to lack imagination and possess a patronising attitude towards Holmes and his methods – seemed to welcome the involvement of the private consulting detective. I have witnessed on more than one occasion that once the official forces work with Holmes and not against him, they invariably come to appreciate his assistance and in some cases, marvel at his expertise.

My reverie was broken and the smile wiped from my face, when I opened the newspaper and read the headline and subsequent article on the inside page.

THEFT AT THE CASTLE
Fenian Activists Suspected

The staggering theft committed last week from the castle remains unsolved. The famous Arroyo Drums, won by the local regiment during the Peninsular War went missing whilst the Commanding Officer Lt. Col. Richard Hulme was attending the Yeomanry camp at Penrith.

It is suspected that Irish Fenians are behind the theft. There has been an upsurge in Irish nationalism recently it is felt that the robbery is the first of many designed to embarrass the authorities. It is feared that this evening's visit by Sir Henry Campbell-Bannerman to the city could also become a target for some form of disruption.

Sergeant Smith of the Cumberland Constabulary has been placed in charge of the case. Earlier today he made the following statement, "We regard this as the most serious of crimes and we will be giving the matter our full attention. I am confident that we will retrieve the drums before the regiment holds its annual parade later this month."

Quite apart from the local policeman's apparent change of attitude towards the crime – no doubt due to the influence of his superior officer – I was mystified as to how the local press had gained access to the story, given that we had only received the 'Irish note' the previous day. I was concerned at this point, as it has been my experience that any kind of involvement by newsmen only succeeds in complicating matters still further. Then it suddenly occurred to me; I would wager that brutish landlord we encountered the previous day had sought to supplement the money handed over by Holmes by making mischief with the local press for further financial reward. The scoundrel! I thought to myself.

As the sky darkened and afternoon ambled towards its daily rendezvous with evening, I returned to the Inn to await Holmes, angry at the barman's apparent betrayal.

A little after six o'clock, Holmes finally returned.

"Where have you been?" I asked.

"You did not notice we were passing Bank Street, the location of Gibson the Tailor's shop?" replied my friend. Prompted by my blank expression, he continued, "I have been to visit your friend Mr. Scott. I must agree with you Watson, he is a most interesting fellow."

I felt somewhat placated by his latter comment after feeling a little foolish by the former. "And what did you learn?" I asked.

"I learned that Mr. Scott picked up an odd number of uniforms for cleaning last week, after the regulars returned from Penrith," he replied, heading for his private bedroom, "oh, and what is more, he has kindly consented to supply us with some clothes for tomorrow evening's adventure."

Not really taking in what he said, I was keen to draw his attention to the newspaper article. "Have you seen the headline?" I said hurriedly, holding up the paper.

"Yes, there was a copy in the shop," he replied with his hand on the doorknob of his room, "an act of desperation I feel." With that he was gone, leaving me standing there, holding the newspaper above my head, perhaps more puzzled than at any other time.

"Now I think we should have a quick bite to eat," said Holmes re-entering our sitting room some moments later, "before joining our professional colleagues in preparation for their VIP visit."

"What do you mean, an act of desperation?" I asked, referring to his previous comment.

"It is not important," was Holmes's infuriating reply.

"Not important?" I echoed, "surely we should not be so blasé about possible activists in the city. Remember those brigands made assassination attempts against our late, great Majesty. With the visit of Sir Henry this evening – as unthinkable as such an eventuality would be – it would surely be negligent of us to disregard the possibility of the same group making a similar attempt on the life of such a high ranking official."

"Good old Watson" – Holmes's tone was kindly, bordering on patronising – "always worrying about others and considering the most outlandish eventuality. You need not concern yourself however, old fellow. I cannot guarantee Sir Henry's visit will run like clockwork, but I am confident that no such attempt will be made on his life. That said, I would not be surprised to find Inspector Armstrong sharing your concerns and as such, we should support his operation, especially when you consider we will be requiring his help prior to our returning to London."

Not altogether convinced about Holmes's assumption and without sharing his confidence, I went down and see Mrs. Graham, who kindly agreed to make us a sandwich at short notice.

A few minutes later, Billy came up carrying a tray, "There you go, gentleman, a couple of me mam's best doorsteps!"

The 'doorsteps' were indeed of finest quality and most welcome fare. We consumed them with great enthusiasm and washed them down with the pot of coffee that accompanied them. Upon completion of our early evening meal, we made our way to the railway station, where a tight security cordon made up of uniform officers met us.

"Sorry sir," said a heavily built young officer, addressing Holmes, "no one beyond this point."

Inspector Armstrong appeared from the entrance to the station. "Let them through Constable," he shouted at his subordinate, "they're on *our* side!"

"Good evening Armstrong, how are your preparations going?" asked Holmes as we approached.

"Terrible – as if I haven't got enough to worry about!" replied the policeman. "I shall be glad when our visitor is safely back on the train heading for London. Do you see these characters from London anywhere Mr. Holmes?"

"No," replied Holmes glancing round casually at the ever-increasing crowd. "You could not fail to spot Mr. Bennett yourself; he is such a distinctive character. As for his associate, I do not think he will be concerning himself with local, or even national politics at this time."

"We saw the report in this evening's paper referring to the Irish activists," said the policeman. "I must say the lads and I are pretty nervous about it. The last thing I want is some clandestine assassination attempt made on such a distinguished character."

"Calm yourself Inspector," countered my friend, smiling at me as his assumptions about Armstrong's thought process had been proved accurate, "there is no need to be so dramatic, I do not believe that will happen. I think you will find the story to be the proverbial 'red herring'. I am more concerned that it is buying the thieves of the Arroyo Drums more time to make their escape. Alas, until I receive a reply to the telegram I send earlier, we are not in a position to do a great deal."

Before Armstrong could reply or I could question Holmes about his theory, there was some activity from within the station entrance.

"What is it?" questioned the Inspector, to a group of uniformed railway personnel.

"Sir Henry's train is slightly early," replied one, "it'll be on the platform in a minute or two."

As the brief conversation was taking place, a carriage that displayed the city's crest on its door pulled up and, rather hurriedly, out stepped a figure dressed in a scarlet cloak with an ermine collar, and a gold link chain draped around his shoulders. His female companion – clad in similar attire – in like manner did not wait for the door to be opened for her as she alighted on the other side of the carriage.

"Mr. Mayor; Lady Mayoress," said Armstrong, saluting as they hastily shot past. The Inspector then looked up to some men he had stationed on the roof of an adjacent hotel, placed there to ensure the rest of his men were in their correct positions and alert to any danger that may occur.

Holmes remained close to the entrance of the station looking quite relaxed about the whole operation. I had the impression he had little interest in the arrival of the VIP but simply agreed to attend out of deference to his professional colleague.

A few minutes later the local dignitaries re-appeared with the impressive figure, I recognised as Sir Henry Campbell-Bannerman, leader of The Liberal Party. As they appeared there was a muffled cheer of acknowledgement from the crowd that loosely lined the cobbled courtyard that naturally measured some fifty yards square in front of the station.

I myself was quite impressed by Sir Henry, having seen him give a speech some twelve months earlier on the merits of forging closer links with our European neighbours after the disastrous prices we had paid in both human and economic terms, as a result of our participation in the South African war.

The party of local and national dignitaries waved from the entrance of the station and posed as a photographer had set his camera up on a tripod between them and the carriage. Standing on the other side of the square, I saw the look of horror on the face of Inspector Armstrong as he watched the photographer preparing his work. Moments later there was a loud cheer from the crowd as the dull 'whoof' of the camera, accompanied by a flash of light and a small explosion of smoke that rose into the darkening sky, signified the successful taking of the picture. The look of relief on the policeman's face was palpable; it was clear the detective was on edge. Already fearing some criminal activity disrupting the occasion, he obviously saw the photographic picture opportunity as an ideal moment for such agitation.

With the local press satisfied, the party then climbed into the carriage and pulled away – flanked by uniformed officers on horseback – up the slight incline in the direction of the town hall, where I believe a light meal was to precede the politician's speech to the local councillors and members of the local guild.

[The party then climbed into the carriage and pulled away]

As the carriage disappeared from our sight, Armstrong rejoined us by the station entrance. "Thank you for your assistance gentlemen, so far, so good. I am always nervous before these things take place. I'm a bit more relaxed once the operation is underway. Security around the town hall is as tight as a drum; no pun intended you understand. Notwithstanding the break-in there at the weekend – something that you have already explained away Mr. Holmes – I am confident the rest of the visit will go smoothly. You are more than welcome to stay and see Sir Henry off gentlemen, but if you prefer, given that it will be around midnight when his train leaves, I am more than happy to handle it from here."

"We will leave you to it then Inspector," replied Holmes. "No doubt we shall meet up again tomorrow evening to address the other problem we appear to have encountered."

"Indeed. I will have a team awaiting your instruction from six o'clock onwards. Until then gentlemen, goodnight and thank you once again."

"Not a bad fellow, Armstrong – just like his cousin," I commented as we made our way back.

"No," agreed Holmes, "we have certainly encountered far worse in his profession during our many adventures."

Magnanimous indeed! I thought to myself.

Chapter Nine

A Dramatic Arrest

Following my friend's final instruction the night before, I rose on the Saturday morning and deliberately avoided my razor; something that would leave me irritable and uncomfortable for the remainder of the day.

"If we are to pass as two working class ruffians," he had said, as we were about to turn in, "we must make every effort to look the part."

Holmes joined me in our sitting room shortly after nine thirty, looking equally unkempt. He looked at me, and I at him, with smiles mirrored on each of our faces telling of our thoughts concerning the other's appearance. We ventured quietly down stairs for some breakfast and then returned to our rooms once more, with the morning paper to wait the appointed hour.

The local newspaper was full of the VIP's visit of the previous evening, with the photograph we ourselves had witnessed being taken outside the station, dominating the front page. Details of Sir Henry's speech were included in the piece that was rounded off with a quote from our new friend, Inspector Armstrong, who was obviously happy the visit had passed off without incident and that '... the danger apparently threatened by Irish Fenians did not materialise'.

"Good old Armstrong," sniped Holmes over my shoulder, "just like the rest of them, he cannot resist getting his name in print."

"Be fair Holmes," I said, "the chap was clearly concerned about the visit and all in all, he seems to have organised the security surrounding it rather well."

A rather less than generous "Hmmm," was all that was forthcoming from my friend.

It was about four o'clock when old Mr. Scott turned up with the clothes we were to use during our evening's adventure.

"I hope these will do the trick gentlemen," he said laying a bundle that was wrapped in brown paper and tied with string, on the chez-long. "They are some of the old clothes we collect, clean and repair before giving them to the Salvation Army who distribute them among the poor folk of the city."

Holmes cut into the bundle and chuckled to himself. He laid out two black heavy-duty waist length workmen's jackets, some old shirts, neckerchiefs, trousers and a couple of flat caps that had seen better days. The old man had even brought two old pairs of boots that fitted perfectly and made our outfits complete.

"These will do nicely my dear Scott, thank you," he said. "I will make sure they are back with you on Monday morning."

We bade the tailor a good afternoon and Holmes set about making the old clothes even more authentic. He called on Billy to take them down to the cellar and "... role around in them for a while!" Upon the lad's return, the detective completed their grubby appearance by tearing at the odd seam here and there and scuffing the boots with the fireside poker. As he was doing so, I was wondering what Scott and his employer would make of the garments upon their return. Holmes then split the clothes up between us and arranged for Mrs. Graham to repeat the repast she made for us the previous evening, prior to our preparing for the commencement of our evening's adventure by retiring to change.

I climbed into my old clothes and was amused as I checked my appearance in the mirror. If I keep my head down, I'm sure I can pass myself off as a labourer, I thought to myself, rubbing my – by now – heavily stubbled chin. Momentarily

Holmes rejoined me in the sitting room. I was absolutely staggered, as my friend had not so much thrown on some old clothes to create an appearance; rather his whole demeanour and personality had altered. If it were possible he had lost over an inch in height, with a slight tilt of the shoulders. He had a hint of soot spattered around his face and his – normally so immaculate – un-creamed hair, flopped down untidily over his forehead. Even though my friend did not have access to his usually considerable resource when taking up one of his infamous disguises, I swear I would have passed him in the street on this occasion, had I not had this sneak preview.

He was equally complimentary about my appearance. Joining me at the mirror he said with a laugh, "Excellent Watson. A couple of more roguish characters I would not wish to meet!"

Holmes then covered once more what he expected to happen over the following few hours. He reminded me that the governor of the County Gaol, Mr. Lyons, would arrange for Simmons and one of his colleagues to be in the, so called, 'Gaol Tap' pub. They would then divulge certain information concerning the arrangements surrounding the transference of Raymond Adams. Holmes's calculated gamble was that one of Adams" accomplices, Styles, would be there; he would pick up on the indiscretion and lead us back to his hideout where both he and his colleague Bennett would be apprehended by Inspector Armstrong and his men.

He suggested that we enter the premises separately as to attract as little attention as possible, "You go in first Watson and find a quiet corner; I'll follow you in after ten minutes or so and we will see how our plan unfolds. Remember Styles and his companion can be dangerous characters, my friend, so we must be on our guard at all times."

With these words of warning ringing in my ears I set off for the City Arms public house.

Recalling my first impressions of the pub as I arrived, and Harry Vaughan's warning – 'You do not want to being hanging around there after dark' – I was filled with trepidation, as I entered. I found the town centre Inn with a not inconsiderable amount of patrons, given that I believed it to be a rather early hour in the evening. I immediately recognised Simmons, the guard from the gaol who we met earlier in the week. He was standing by the bar with a colleague and although they had top coats on, their prison uniforms were clear for all to see under the unbuttoned over garments. I wondered if that was for effect during this operation or, bearing in mind Governor Lyon's reservations about his men frequenting such an establishment, it was normal practice.

*[The City Arms or 'Gaol Tap',
where we passed unrecognised]*

I walked over to the bar and mustered up my best attempt at the local dialect by barking, "Give uz a pint," at the poor chap behind the bar. To my astonishment, the barman – obviously used to being spoken to in such a discourteous manner – responded to my demand without a second glance. Furthermore, the two guards standing nearby did not react, or even appear to recognise me. My inward cringing turned to smug satisfaction as I took my drink and walked towards a vacant table in one corner of the establishment. I sat down, pulled down my cap and waited.

Some minutes later Holmes made his entrance. As I stated earlier, had I not had prior warning of my friend's appearance, I would never have recognised him. Every aspect of his manner and behaviour was completely in keeping with our surroundings. The scene I myself acted out moments earlier was repeated but I was sure Holmes was far more natural and convincing in the role. After being served, he sidled over to a stool at the far end of the bar and slumped down over his drink.

It was sometime after six thirty when the reason for our presence materialised. A pitiable figure of a man, not so much walked, as shuffled his way through the doors of the Inn and towards the bar. His sever disability was plain for all to see and even with my considerable experience of most medical matters, and as well as being fully aware of the man's villainous background, I could not help feeling some sorrow for this individual. That notwithstanding, this was clearly our man and Holmes's warning about this deceptively dangerous character remained with me, as I concentrated on the matter in question.

Although Styles's arrival caught the attention of some of the clientele within the establishment, I felt this was due simply to his apparent incapacity than to any other significant reason. I was conscious however, that Simmons visibly tensed when he saw the criminal enter, and foolishly nudged his colleague as if to forewarn him of the impending act they were to play out. Holmes, of course – still seated at the other end of the bar – did not flicker at the appearance of his quarry. Fortunately, Styles did not see Simmons" give-away sign and carried on about his business, taking a tankard of ale from the bar and making for a table.

From my position in the bar room I had the perfect vantage point from which to observe every element of the scene that was about to unfold. The patrons of the increasingly crowded pub carried on about their business, completely unaware that their place of relaxation was the stage on which this pre-arranged drama was about to be played out.

No sooner had Styles left the bar, than Simmons – in a slightly raised voice to make him heard above the escalating background noise – said to his colleague, "That's a rum do about that Adams bloke, mind you."

The villain stopped in his tacks, unobserved by anyone who would not have known the significance of the comment. He immediately changed direction and headed for a seat that would give him a better opportunity of overhearing the conversation between the two off duty prison wardens.

"What was that then?" said the other guard, taking the lead from his colleague.

"Well there was some carry on, wasn't there? They've moved him over to Durham," continued Simmons, trying desperately not to over-act.

"I thought that wasn't taking place until later."

"Well I don't know much about it, other than it's been brought forward and he's gone already."

As I observed the scene from under the peak of my pulled down cap, I saw Styles's eyes widen as his agitation increased and the realisation of his predicament dawned on him. Clearly his own vulnerability, and that of his colleague, was now overtaking his desire to free his leader. In his haste to vacate the premises and get to Bennett as soon as he could, he rose from his seat and stumbled into a neighbouring table, upsetting some of the drinks in the process, much to the cheering amusement of everyone else in the pub.

"Get out of it, ye bloody menace," cried one of the men sitting at the table, as he pushed him back onto his feet.

The fretting Styles scuttled out of the building. To those of us who knew of the background to the incident, it was obvious that he was not so much worried about the spilled drinks, but the ever-increasing possibility of losing his own liberty.

As he disappeared through the doors back onto the street outside, Holmes – who all the while, had been part of the background, as he sat quietly in his position – calmly got up and walked towards the door himself. I followed his lead and as we walked passed, my friend gave Simmons a friendly slap of acknowledgement on the back. The sudden realisation in the warden's face, that he and his colleague's woeful amateur dramatics had not been in vain after all, was something to behold. It was clear that he was not aware of our presence; something that, I must confess, gave me a great thrill.

Once in the street, Holmes pulled me into the shadows as a precaution against being spotted by our prey, although I was confident that this was not the main thing on Styles's mind as he made his way north through the city centre.

"So far, so good, Watson. I suggest you now go to collect Armstrong and his men while I follow Styles. It is clear he is heading north across the river and as long as the Inspector has his men ready – as he claimed they would be – I am sure you will overtake me before we reach their hide-away."

I followed Holmes's instructions and made my way discretely towards the police station. As arranged, the Inspector was waiting with eight uniformed officers, ready to arrest the criminals from London. Disregarding Armstrong's amusement at my appearance – something I must confess I had forgotten about as the adrenaline had started to pump through my veins – I quickly recounted what had happened so far and invited him and his men to accompany me and join Holmes in the chase for the remaining members of the Adams gang.

Almost as soon as we left the police station, I saw Holmes in the distance, as he kept a long lead on his prey. Some two hundred yards ahead of the detective was the pathetic, struggling figure of Styles as he crossed one of the two bridges that spanned the River Eden and joined the road that headed north up a steep bank towards what I had learned from the farmer, Jennings, as Etterby village. Half way up the bank there was a fork in the road. As we hurried to catch up Holmes, Armstrong informed me that the main road led off to Scotland, while the road that forked to the right was the main eastward road towards Newcastle.

"It was probably around here that the two planned to ambush the vehicle transporting Adams to Durham," concluded the policeman.

Sure enough, as we joined Holmes on the bridge up ahead, we saw Styles peel off in the easterly direction. The river gurgled idly beneath us.

"Keep those policemen out of sight," hissed Holmes, over its noise, obviously fearing failure as the chase reached its climax.

Armstrong instructed his men to hold back as the three of us continued to follow Styles at a discrete distance. As the road levelled there was a sharp turning to the left; this obviously had a steep gradient as it rose to meet the northern road. To the right, the ground fell away to open parkland through which the city's main river ran. We watched carefully, making sure we were out of sight, as Styles, glancing furtively over his shoulder darted up the lane to the left and then along another smaller opening half way up, on the right.

"That'll be Jennings" farm over there," whispered Armstrong pointing, "we can't be far away now."

"I suggest you call your men forward and position them at each end of the lane," said Holmes to the Inspector.

This was done and our wait commenced.

The time was now after eight o'clock and the temperature must have been down around zero. The street lighting was poor; bulbous gas lamps that were positioned approximately one hundred yards apart, failed miserably in their purpose – only succeeding in laying down soft pools of illumination within a four feet radius at the base of their respective posts. Thankfully the full moon that sat serenely in the otherwise black cloudless sky overlooked the eyrie silence in this remote part of the city and afforded sufficient visibility for our covert operation.

After what seemed an eternity, two figures – silhouetted in the moonlight – appeared at the far end of the lane. Although nothing more than featureless black shapes, their identities could not have been in question. The shuffling, uncomfortable gait of Styles was unmistakable, while his companion appeared to be a giant of a man, even at the distance of sixty or more paces. His size was not only exaggerated by his broadness, but also by the comparison to his physically challenged friend, who struggled to keep up with him.

After scurrying half way down the lane the smaller silhouette stopped, sensing something was amiss, and indicated that his companion do the same by reaching up and putting a hand on his forearm. Both stood there, dead still for a moment, their breath visible in the night air; the bigger man snorting like a great Pamplonan bull after his hasty exit from their hideaway.

Holmes, Armstrong and I stood – unseen by our two opponents – watching as they pondered their next move. If it were possible, the tension was increased as owl hooted in the distant parkland and our three heads instinctively turned in silent synchronisation. Seconds seemed like minutes as the combined feeling of suspense and expectancy became almost unbearable.

Finally, Holmes indicated action by placing his hand gently on the shoulder of Inspector Armstrong. The shrill of the senior policeman's whistle instantaneously broke the agonising silence as it echoed up and down the dark lane. In what was a deafening cacophony, uniformed officers made their noisy charge out from their hiding places to apprehend the villains.

Styles's arrest was a formality; he could offer no resistance against the two younger, fitter men who made a grab for him. His accomplice's ability to resist arrest was however, altogether more successful. The policeman nearest to him was sent spinning across the cobbles, with a thunderous right hand. A colleague moved in from the side only to receive an uppercut to the jaw that saw his helmet fly into the air. Two more leaped on the giant's back and, as he whirled them round; windmilling arms and legs became indistinguishable as the misshapen silhouette created almost a comic sight.

*[It was to the rear of these buildings
that we made our dramatic arrest]*

I heard the ripping of cloth as the policemen, in trying to grab their opponent, only succeeded in tearing his coat and then his shirt. We moved forward to just a few paces and it was then that I saw Bennett's bulging naked chest and almost bestial, facial expression. The two officers, previously dispatched by the former boxer, recovered sufficiently and bravely went for him again. They grabbed him by the arms but this still did not deter the huge man from putting up a defence.

"Go on Boom Boom!" yelled the captured Styles as the constables failed to gain the upper hand.

"Round the legs," I heard myself mumbling, sensing that Armstrong was sharing my frustration, as the negligence of his officers unnecessarily delayed the arrest of the villain.

As policemen appeared to be hanging off every face of this man mountain, I could resist the urge no more. Remembering my rugby days at Blackheath, I shot out from the group observing the struggle and raced at the mass of bodies. Diving full length and hitting the knees of Bennett with my shoulder, assailant and the attached policemen came crashing down in a snarling, thrashing heap.

As the villain whirled about twisting on the ground, one poor officer flipped like a cat and fell on the enormous blood splattered back of the giant and was spread-eagled there like a human sacrifice upon the alter. In doing so however, he inadvertently brought the criminal under control and his colleagues managed finally to secure an arrest.

Holmes came running up as giddy as a schoolboy, "Watson, you old scoundrel!" he cried, "this was never part of the plan!" He howled with laughter and, dare I say, admiration at my action.

For my part I was already beginning to regret my decision to bring the fracas to an end. As I lay on the ground, peering up at my friend and Inspector Armstrong, who were both standing over me in wonderment, I felt a searing pain shoot through my previously wounded shoulder and, far from basking in the glory of my action, that brought the chase to its exciting climax, it took all of my composure to refrain from crying out in agony.

Holmes and Armstrong helped me to my feet as the uniformed officers bound Bennett, who was still scrambling about on the ground in what was now futile resistance.

"I cannot thank you gentlemen enough," said the senior policeman, "you have not only solved one crime but prevented another and helped my colleagues at Scotland Yard to complete the apprehension of the whole gang. I would be honoured if you would accompany us back to the station where I will arrange a small celebration," he added tapping the side of his nose.

"It is our pleasure, my dear Inspector, and thank you for your kind offer," replied Holmes, "my friend and colleague has certainly earned his brandy and soda tonight!" With this final comment, Holmes slapped me on the back in triumph and I squeaked with discomfort as the impact shot upward through my shoulder once more. I held my poise however by looking forward to the aforementioned refreshment and the hot bath, I was determined would follow it.

Chapter Ten

An Interlude

I must say I enjoyed our stiff drink back in the Inspector's office and from a medicinal point of view, it also helped numb the throbbing pain in my shoulder. It was clear that the Inspector was delighted with the evening's events.

"I shall call Inspector Gregson tomorrow and inform him of our success," he said. "I have also summoned a reporter from the local newspaper down to give him a scoop for the morning edition."

"I would appreciate it if you would keep our names out of the paper, Inspector," said Holmes characteristically.

"But, Mr. Holmes, if it were not through the efforts of yourself and Doctor Watson, we would never have caught the villains. In fact I would still be on the wild goose chase, believing the thefts at the castle and the town hall were linked, not to mention the resource I would have wasted, as a result of the bogus threat to the cathedral."

"My dear Armstrong, as my trusty biographer here will tell you, it has never been my intention to court sensation and recognition in the press. The successful conclusion of any case is all I crave. No; please feel free to take full credit for the capture of Styles and Bennett – it will do your career no harm I would imagine."

Holmes was clearly in a good mood, after all of the excitement and he continued in such a disposition mood for the next half hour or so, until the reporter from the *Carlisle*

Journal turned up. We made a polite exit at this point and left Armstrong to provide the journalist with the new lead story for the morning paper.

Once in our rooms I climbed into the steaming hot bath I had promised myself, in an attempt to soak away my aches and pains. Despite the lateness of the hour, I even treated myself to a shave, given that it had been thirty-six hours since my chin had seen a razor. By the time I had rejoined the chuckling Holmes by the fire for a nightcap, it was drawing towards midnight.

"Well that is it for me, old fellow," said I, as I drained my glass of its final mouthful, "I shall see you in the morning."

"Good night," said Holmes and, as I reached the door to my room he added, "and Watson? Very good work tonight; thank you."

As I have stated many times in the past, Holmes's manner frequently bordered on the cold, so this final comment almost amounted to a show of affection from my friend. I turned in that night completely worn out but at the same time, extremely contented with my efforts and the appreciation in which both Holmes and Armstrong held them.

One thing I had forgotten to do of course, before retiring, was to check with Holmes on our progress against our primary case and as a result, I failed to arrange any morning call. It was the pealing of the nearby cathedral bells therefore, that woke me as they signified the imminent service at the eleventh hour of the morning.

As I made the effort to get up, the previous evening's adventure immediately came back to me as was overcome by tremendous stiffness in what seemed like every muscle. I felt a shooting pain in my shoulder and once more, questioned the wisdom of my action that brought the struggle to an end. I managed to haul myself out of bed however, washed, shaved and entered our sitting room. Although my friend was not in our communal room, I heard him pottering about in his bedroom, so in his absence I took the opportunity of popping down stairs to collect a selection of the morning papers and arranging some late morning refreshment with our extremely patient and obliging hostess, Mrs. Graham.

I returned to find Holmes smoking a pipe by the fire. I sensed his jovial mood from the previous night had deserted him as my jolly "Good morning," was greeted with a barely audible grunt.

"What are our intentions today?" I asked.

"Nothing until I receive a reply from my telegram."

"Telegram?" I questioned.

"Do keep up Watson," Holmes replied curtly, "the telegram I sent to London on Friday."

My heroics of last night and the subsequent appreciation shown were short lived, I thought to myself philosophically. Thankfully at that point there was a knock at the door and Mrs. Graham entered with a pot of coffee and some eggs, bacon and toast. I tucked into the hearty late breakfast with gusto, while Holmes took just a cup of coffee to accompany his pipe.

It was clear my roommate was in a pensive, non-talkative state of mind. Furthermore, I knew that even if I could entice him out of this, I would undoubtedly have discovered him in one of his more disputatious moods. I therefore decided to leave him to it and settle down to read the morning journals, obviously interested most in how the local paper reported the exciting events of the previous evening.

'CITY ARREST OF LONDON CRIMINALS!' was the dramatic title of the piece that outlined the apprehension of Styles and Bennett. A thorough summary then followed into the background of the Adams gang, with their various successes and failures being listed. An outline of the reason for their presence in Carlisle was given, with appropriate quotes from Inspector Armstrong and even the lugubrious Governor Lyons, giving the piece credibility. One of Armstrong's more generous, if cryptic quotes, referred to the '... considerable assistance given by two members of the public, who acted above and beyond what is expected of any private citizen. I have no doubt that these arrests could not have been effected successfully, had it not been for their help'.

"Good man, Armstrong!" I said to myself, acknowledging our help and yet adhering to Holmes's request to keep our names out of the paper. Holmes of course, showed little interest in our joint triumph but continued to gaze into the crackling fire.

Another hour of this inactive Sabbath past, and then another and with it, Holmes's agitation increased. Although there was clearly danger the previous night in our apprehending of the London criminals, retrospectively I was glad there was something to occupy that great mind of his, as the primary reason for our presence here seemed to be dragging on somewhat.

Ordinarily, had Holmes been locked away in his Baker Street den, I'm sure his attention would have drifted towards the cocaine bottle, as this was his usual protest against the tedium of existence. I do believe however, that this dreadful vice was not so much an addiction but a substitute for the adrenaline created by the thrilling chase, the excitement of discovery and the activity of detection.

For my part I must confess to missing my own hearth and my dear wife tremendously during these periods of inactivity. I broke the tedium by reading the Sunday newspaper and writing up details of the case to date.

By three o'clock in the afternoon, Holmes was like a caged animal once more, prowling round our quarters. If he was not biting his nails, he was grinding his teeth and when he was doing neither of these, he would stand on the hearthrug, frowning, eyes tightly closed, while his fingers would drum like pistons upon the mantelpiece, as if fingering one of the great violin masterpieces he so admired. During this period he appeared to smoke endless cigarettes. The heightening tension was finally broken by a knock at the door that pre-empted young Billy's entrance to our quarters with a telegram.

"At last!" cried Holmes, ripping open the missive and almost instantaneously giving a snort of disapproval.

"What is it?" I asked.

"Gregson!" barked Holmes, virtually throwing the message at me.

The message ran thus:

ARMSTRONG ADVISED ME OF STYLES AND BENNETT ARREST STOP THANK YOU FOR YOUR CONTINUED ASSISTANCE STOP BRANDY AND CIGARS ON ME WHEN YOU RETURN END TOBIAS GREGSON

Whereas I acknowledged the Scotland Yard Detective's genuine intent and thanks, Holmes cast it aside as he viewed it as a distraction from the case in hand. I escorted Billy back out on to the landing outside our room and asked, "Is there anywhere I could take Mr. Holmes on a Sunday afternoon that would help relieve his boredom?"

"Well sir, the brass bands 've finished in the park last month for the summer. Mind you the fun fair's still on!" was the youngster's enthusiastic reply.

I laughed at the thought of Sherlock Holmes killing a few hours at the various stalls, rides and mirrored hallways offered by the lad's suggestion. "Hardly appropriate," I said.

"The only other thing's the baths then," concluded Billy

"Baths? Is there a Turkish bath?"

"Yes sir, on James Street. Just go down English Street and across the viaduct, you'll see it on the left hand side."

I gave the boy a shilling for his help and his deliverance of the telegram, took a deep breath and re-entered our room, prepared to make my suggestion.

"Holmes you have been a veritable bear all day, I suggest we go out and try to find some relaxation."

"What do you have in mind," asked my friend, his expression lightening somewhat.

"The young lad tells me that there is a Turkish bath nearby; I think it is just the solution to our aches and pains, not to mention re-invigorating the old grey matter!"

Looking around at the increasingly thick atmosphere of our room, Holmes replied, "Anything to beat this endless stagnation I suppose. Watson, what would I do without you?"

On what was now a rather muggy afternoon, we donned our outdoor-wear once more and followed the young lad's directions, crossing the Victoria Viaduct in the process, which – according to the plaque at its central point – was opened and named in honour of her mother by Princess Louise during her visit to the city in 1877.

Upon entering the public baths we paid the young lady on the front desk who directed us along a corridor to the Turkish bath. There, we found ourselves in surroundings as far removed from an industrial city in the north of England as could be imagined. The tasteful Moorish decor was complimented beautifully by the palms and tropical plants that were strategically arranged throughout the spacious entrance area.

A Turkish Bath was a treat my friend and I regularly enjoyed and I was pleasantly surprised that such a facility was available to us; not only could we indulge ourselves in such a pleasant pastime, but it also broke up the interminably boring day.

After our invigorating bath, Holmes and I spent a relaxing period in the high temperature and moist atmosphere of the steam area, before rapping ourselves in crisp white sheets and spending another equally enjoyable hour over a pipe in the drying room. Our usual haunt in Northumberland Avenue had a hookah that Holmes enjoyed inhaling, but a relaxing pipe whilst allowing our pores to breathe and cleans was most acceptable to us both.

I was delighted with my suggestion that brought us out of our quarters; my remaining stiffness from the previous night's activity, not to mention the pain in my shoulder, was gradually eradicated as our relaxing afternoon wore on. I even sensed that Holmes was finally beginning to wind down from his earlier agitated state, although we both sat in silence throughout.

We stepped back into our lodgings as the quarter hour before seven struck on the town hall clock opposite. Upon our entrance Mr. Graham once again produced a second telegram addressed to Holmes, who opened it instantly.

My friend omitted a soft velvet "Ahhh; just as I suspected."

"What is it?" I asked as we climbed the stairs.

"Brother Mycroft!" was all Holmes would divulge.

"Mycroft?" I said, as we entered our suite, "What has Mycroft got to do with this?"

"He is rather slow and cumbersome," he said, "but as ever, he is extremely reliable and his contacts are invaluable." Stopping at the door of his bedroom he added, "I do believe all of the data I require is now available to me. I have now to analyse it." With that cryptic comment, he was gone.

I resumed my reading of the papers for sometime before deciding to go downstairs for something to eat. Knowing the answer beforehand, but asking the question out of courtesy anyway, I shouted "Will you be joining me for dinner Holmes?"

"No, you carry on Watson, I have to formulate the data gathered," came his reply.

As I left our rooms I virtually bumped into Captain Vaughan, who was just about to knock on our door. "Harry! What a pleasant surprise. What brings you here?"

"Good evening old man, I was just interested to see what the latest position was regarding the case," said my former colleague, "the colonel is becoming increasingly concerned."

"Well, perhaps you would like me to join me for dinner and we could discuss it," I said. In making the offer I must confess that I was hoping more for a dining companion rather than the opportunity of analysing the theft of the Spanish Drums, for in my heart I knew I did not have much to discuss!

To my relief and genuine delight, Vaughan consented to my offer and we went down stairs to sample our hostess' considerable culinary talents.

During our meal we discussed many issues starting almost inevitably with the weather. Vaughan explained how his colleague and erstwhile cousin of the Police Inspector, Sergeant Armstrong, was something of an amateur meteorological expert

"He can see a storm coming days in advance," said the army officer, "which is very useful in the field. I sometimes think he would have been more suited to the navy than the army," he added, laughing. "Told me earlier he expects a 'belter' tonight and he is very rarely incorrect in his meteorological predictions."

From there our conversation drifted once more back to Afghanistan to the relative boredom of civilian life and even to his reminding me of his distant relationship with Lennard Stokes, my old rugby playing captain, who went on to play for England.

"Of course!" I cried, "dear old Stokes, what a player he was. How is he doing these days?"

"Sadly he passed away some years ago. His career ended through injury and from there his health gradually deteriorated."

With the raising of the subject of Rugby Football, I was reminded of our adventure the previous evening, and I shared with Vaughan the series of events that culminated with my recreating my best centre three quarter's tackle. We both laughed at the folly of my actions.

"We are getting too old for such activity, John," said my friend.

Our laughter faded and I decided to broach the delicate issue that had been niggling at the back of my mind since Holmes's interview with Sergeant Armstrong, "Tell me Harry, what do you make of the new RSM?"

"Former Northumberland Fusilier, like yourself!" was his jovial reply.

"Yes I know but how does the man strike you? He seems quite a strange type to me and everyone seems rather non committal when talking about him."

"Be fair Watson, the man has only been with us a few weeks. I agree that he behaves rather unusually for one in his position but I just put it down to him finding his feet."

"Perhaps you are right," I said, admittedly unconvinced. As I had broken the ice however, in discussing some of the military personnel, I decided to press the matter further by risking the touching of a nerve with Vaughan by bringing up another of his colleagues; "And Major Young?"

"Clive? Oh he's all right. Sometimes gets a little full of himself but I think he will make a decent Major in time."

"Yes, Holmes and I experienced his rather haughty attitude the other day; made a bit of a fool of himself given that he was in charge of the depot while the theft occurred." I was impressed at the magnanimity of my former colleague, having learned from Sergeant Armstrong that Young had beaten him to the promotion earlier in the year.

"Well, we all make mistakes, I suppose," he said.

"Are you sorry for your colleague's predicament or your failure to secure the promotion?"

"Perhaps a little bit of both," he answered with a rueful smile.

As we enjoyed a cigar and a brandy after our most enjoyable meal, the thunderstorm that had been predicted by Vaughan's NCO colleague, hit the county city.

"I had better make a dash for it, old fellow," said my dining companion, draining his glass and reaching for his army issue raincoat. "Until tomorrow then," he said reaching out a hand.

"Good night Harry, you had better be quick, it's fairly building up out there."

He made his hasty exit and I sat alone for a while and finished my drink, pondering the rather pleasant evening I had enjoyed with my old friend and the subjects we had covered during our conversation.

"Did you enjoy that sir?" I came back to life with a start as our hostess addressed me, whilst she cleared our table.

"I did indeed Mrs. Graham, another superb meal. Thank you. You are certainly kept busy," I said continuing the conversation, "you must be worn out."

"Yes, there's no stopping in this job, Doctor. But ye get used to it, I suppose. Sleep well now," she said as she left the table loaded down with dishes.

"Good night, and thank you again."

It was ten thirty by the time I left my table and as I climbed the stairs of our diggings I was content with in the knowledge that I would be soon in our snug chamber and equally, that I did not have to venture out on such a night as this. As I reached our rooms the weather conditions had reached Wagnerian proportions. I entered to find our suite in darkness, save for the intermittent brilliance created by the flashes of light from the storm outside. I gave a start as I realised I was not alone in the room. Holmes – in his purple dressing gown – was perched on some pillows and cushions in one corner of the room with his eyes closed and his clay pipe between his lips. Although I had seen him in this pose before, the sudden realisation of his presence made my heart skip a beat. I walked over to the window to watch the storm. It was in itself like a fierce military assault, with loud cannonade of thunder, a fusillade of rain and hail on the window, whilst in the distance the medieval castle appeared to be under attack from the swords of lightning that erupted from the angry skies above.

I turned to look at my friend, who came into view every time the room was illuminated by the blue and yellow electric flashes. He sat there throughout, in eyrie silence, apparently oblivious to my presence and the violence outside. I knew it was futile to disturb him so I decided to turn in and try and get some sleep.

"Good night old fellow" I said, leaving him to what I knew would be an all night sitting.

Chapter Eleven

An Interview With The Harbourmaster

As I opened my bedroom window the following morning, I found the air to be far fresher than that of the previous day – obviously due to the thunderstorm that raged on, well into the night. I indulged in several deep breaths of this crisp air before making my way towards our sitting room.

When I entered I was overcome by the dramatic change in atmosphere; the room was full of black acrid smoke! It immediately dawned on me that this was a legacy from Holmes's all-nighter, and his smoking of endless pipe-fulls of his favourite dark shag tobacco. Before I could rebuke myself for having forgotten about how I had left my friend the previous evening, and then for my subsequent lack of preparedness, I exploded into an uncontrollable coughing fit. Reaching for my handkerchief and placing it over my mouth, I made my way over to the window, waving the air with the other hand, in a futile effort to disperse the dense pollution.

I raised the sash and took some more deep breaths of the morning air, albeit it in a less relaxed manner than that of a few minutes earlier, when in my own room. I must have made a comical sight from the street outside, hanging out of the window gasping for air while smoke billowed out from behind me.

When I had regained a little more composure and the air had cleared somewhat I shouted, "Holmes? Holmes, are your awake?" admittedly part in retaliation for my companion catching me off guard. No reply was forthcoming from his room and at that moment an envelope on the mantle-piece caught my eye, simply marked 'WATSON'. Upon opening the envelope, I found the contents to be equally brief; the note simply read:

> Gone to Silloth!
>
> SH

I assumed Holmes was continuing his investigation, but I must confess to being somewhat piqued at his ambiguous message and the fact that he had seen fit to apparently progress his enquiries without me. I went down for breakfast pondering over the vaguely familiar place-name.

Mr. Graham greeted me, and I asked him, "Who, or what is Silloth?"

"Silloth sir? That's our local holiday resort, about twenty-five miles west of Carlisle. The beaches out there are lovely in the summer," the local man added, enthusiastically.

I snapped my finger in sudden realisation, "Of course!" I said, as much to myself as to our host, 'I remember now; Sergeant Armstrong mentioned it when we spoke with him on Friday.'

I spent the rest of my morning meal trying to follow Holmes's thought process that led him to go to the seaside resort, without much success I must confess.

As my friend was away and had left me no instructions to carry out in his absence, I left the Inn that morning a little at a loss as to how to spend my time. I ambled aimlessly around the nearby cathedral grounds before ending up at the public library that was located further down Castle Street at its mid-point, between the two historic buildings.

Inside, my eye wandered toward the local history section and almost inevitably rested upon a book about the castle itself; its background, history and the various adventures it had experienced.

[*Carlisle Cathedral*]

I removed my hat and coat, found an easy chair and read with fascination about the great red triangular fortress with its classic outlook; set as it is, on a hill facing north over the River Eden to confront the enemy, in the shape of the barbarous Picts and Scots.

Centuries earlier Roman soldiers had been sent to the area to augment their leaders' boundaries. Indeed, only yards from where I was sitting – in the grounds of the library – there was evidence of a working aqueduct that had been built by the Romans. Legionnaires, who had come from far and wide to fight, will undoubtedly have cursed the bitter conditions, marooned, as they were on this key fortress adjacent to the Emperor Hadrian's Great Wall. I chuckled to myself at the thought of a group of Roman soldiers, based in some beautifully warm Mediterranean province, being approached by their Centurion: "All right men, I've just been advised of a new posting for us ..."

This was *their* Northwest Frontier.

When Rome fell, Dark Age chieftains, perhaps even King Arthur among them – the piece suggested that the nearby Isle of Man was his Avalon – used the remains and ruins of the castle for their own wars. The eleventh century then saw William II rebuilt the fortification, apparently incorporating mythical passageways and channels in the process, which alas, only resulted in the castle becoming the focus of over five hundred further years of bloody warfare between the English and the Scots. William Wallace, Robert the Bruce and the Jacobite army led by Bonnie Prince Charlie all viewed Carlisle Castle – vulnerable as it was, only eight miles from their own border – as England's first great prize.

Kings of Scotland had been crowned there and legendary warriors executed there. Richard the Lionheart used the Northern Marshes as his training ground; the same marshes where, over eighty years later, Edward I died as he advanced to face Robert the Bruce.

I read with continued fascination about how – in the 16th century – the castle had witnessed the infamous Border Reivers; men from counties on both sides of the border whose circumstances constrained them to earn a living by robbing and plundering others. In reading about these men, I was intrigued to read of their family names – Armstrong, Graham, Scott, and Nixon among them – all characters whose descendants we had encountered during our visit. I was thrilled to learn that my own surname was also an associate Reiver name, although I am not sure if I would have been as thrilled to meet that certain branch of my family tree!

Not only had the stronghold acted as a backdrop to the adventures of the Reivers, but it was also a prison for Mary Queen of Scots, who was held in the very tower that was named after her; the same tower from which the drums were stolen.

I learned that the castle was also the subject of a siege during the civil war and for the last two hundred years it had been used as the depot from which the local regiment would leave to fight all over the Empire.

*[Castle Street, looking towards the Castle with the
clock tower of Tullie House on the left]*

This was wonderful stuff! I thought to myself. I had spent a
most enjoyable morning educating myself on the local subject
and concluded that the perpetrators of the theft of the drums
must have discovered one of William II's passageways in the
underbelly of the fortress and made their cunning escape into
the blackness of the night. It was shortly before one o'clock
when I left the library to walk the short distance to the Crown
and Mitre. I could not wait to share my theory with Holmes
upon his return. I had barely been in our rooms five minutes
when my friend entered with a flourish.

"Good afternoon Watson, my boy! What a beautiful day!"

"Holmes, what have you been doing?"

"I have been breathing in over five hours of Cumberland's finest coastal air this morning and I am famished!" was his infuriatingly ambiguous reply, "I will tell you all about it over lunch."

At our table, before Holmes could resume his narrative, I ventured to put forward my theory after my morning's education.

"Watson, you could not be further from the truth," said my friend. "You are a romantic, my dear fellow and this, combined with a writer's imagination has led you away from the facts."

"What is your suggestion then?" I asked.

"I am already aware of how the crime was committed and, more importantly who committed it, but the capture of the criminals and recovery of stolen items is in the balance."

Holmes then went through the series of events that led us to our current position.

"You left me last evening pondering the state of the case and the evidence that was available to us. I must say I found the combination of our relaxing Sunday afternoon and last night's thunderstorm quite stimulating. I think the latter succeeded in finally hammering some sense into me!

"Our interview with Sergeant Armstrong on Friday morning was most informative and I decided that the best escape route for the criminals was by sea. This way they could flee, virtually at their own pace, while the authorities would almost certainly cover the road and rail outlets."

"But what was the significance of the telegram you received from Mycroft?" I interrupted.

"The theft of the Arroyo Drums was so unusual," answered Holmes, "that I believed the background to it would lay in the history of the trophies themselves. Until I received confirmation of this theory from Mycroft, I could not act upon it. Putting this information together with the other details we have received so far, it led me to the seaside town and industrial shipping outlet of Silloth. I sat for most of the night waiting for the early morning train."

"Yes, I nearly choked on the room full of tobacco smoke you left behind," I said.

[*Silloth Docks, where Holmes made a discovery*]

"I caught the five thirty-two from Carlisle," he continued, ignoring my comment, "and found myself by the seaside within the hour. I explained to the conductor on the way that I was looking for information concerning traffic in and out of the docks and he advised me to speak with Anderson, the

Harbourmaster, who knows 'everything there is to know about the comings and goings in this part of the world'. Upon our arrival, the railway official gave me directions to the docks and I set off in search of this nautical sage.

"Once at the harbour, I perceived a lone figure on the otherwise deserted quayside. Perched on one of the bollards that stood like soldiers along the docking area was a rotund figure, with a weathered complexion and a white beard that matched the hair protruding from under his seaman's cap. He sat, looking out at the subject that, no doubt, had dominated his life, enjoying an early morning pipe.

"'Mr. Anderson I presume,' I called.

"'Mornin', bit early for you city types,' replied the old man, eyeing me up and down.

"'Isle-o-Man Ferry doesn't leave till ten o'clock'."

Not only was Holmes a master of disguise, he had the ability to mimic most dialects after the briefest of meetings. Always a lover of the dramatic in such situations, he did not hesitate in adopting the Cumberland accent as he recited his tale to me.

"'I am not here for the ferry Mr. Anderson. My name is Sherlock Holmes and I have been commissioned by the Border Regiment to look into a theft from Carlisle Castle'.

"'That's a new 'un,' Anderson said laughing, 'how can I help?'

"'I have reason to believe that the thieves made their getaway by sea. Given the direct access to Silloth and its closer proximity to Carlisle than, say, Whitehaven or Maryport, I suspect that they chose this location from which to leave the county'.

"'If it's the same blokes I'm thinking of, you're right in thinking they chose Silloth, but I can tell ye that they ended up going by the railway'.

"I sat down with Anderson and shared a pipe with him. I enlightened him as to the details of the case and, more importantly, the various dates on which we believe each event took place.

"'Aye that'll be about right,' he said, 'they turned up and harboured their steamer about ten days ago. One of them told me that they intended to leave with some cargo from Carlisle a week gone Tuesday, sailing at midnight. Of course they never made it did they? The storm saw to that. Wrecked their boat and three others that were moored alongside it overnight.

"'It was clear that they wanted to get away quick, coz they were fair panicking when the storm hit. They were all for taking their chance before I held them back. I wasn't gonna let anyone go out in that weather'.

"He took me over to an adjoining yard, where the wrecked boats were. I saw for myself the damage incurred by the boats on the night in question and bearing in mind that this damage had occurred while they were in the harbour, it would have been the folly indeed to have made a dash for it, given the condition of the steamer as I saw it. That particular night was certainly not one for mariners and undoubtedly, the vessel and all its hands would not have stood a chance on the open sea.

"'What did they do?' I then asked Anderson.

"'As I say, they were desperate. When a told them a wasn't gonna let them go, the one who did all the talking asked if there was a shed they could use to store their cargo. There's plenty of storage in the warehouses ova yonder,' he said, pointing, 'so a told him they could use one of them. Then they moved the crates over to where I directed them and stored them in the corner of one of the houses. Three o' them insisted on staying wid the cargo, while the talker buggered off!'

"'They stayed with the crates?' I repeated.

"'Aye,' replied the local man, roaring with laughter, as he offered to show me, 'they had a long wait mind you. A different one disappeared every night while the other two kipped down in the warehouse. It wasn't till yesterday that the talker turned up and asked if they could move their cargo. He told me they were gonna tek it by train after all'.

"Sure enough, in the warehouse, there were clear signs of recent occupation. Fortunately for the detective, the sandy base of the building allowed plenty of tracks to be created. The group did not feel it necessary to cover the marks and had I not have already known that there were four of them, I could have easily deduced it from the differing footprints."

"Four?" I questioned.

Holmes continued, ignoring my interruption, "Those I believed to have been from the leader of the group were fewer that those of his colleagues, confirming Anderson's testimony that he went missing for some days. I assumed that the members of the gang that remained took turns to spend a night each in their lodgings, while his two colleagues remained with the drums. This was confirmed when I discovered later when I made some discrete house to house enquiries along the sea front houses that indicated available accommodation. Sure enough, the landlady of one of the establishments informed me that the four men had stayed with her at various times over the past week, and whereas she was aware that they were together, they never actually stayed in her lodgings as a group, 'Strange bunch if y'ask me', was her only contribution to the conversation.

"Back in the warehouse, it was also obvious to the naked eye as to where the crates containing the drums had been stacked. I suggest there were three, as two had made obvious indentations in the sand, but each impression was deeper on each adjacent side. Suggestion? That a third container was placed on top of, but spanning the other two.

"'Did the leader of the group tell you where he went during his absence?' I asked Anderson.

"'Well no he didn't, but I would guess, he'd be making arrangements to go to Liverpool, if they still wanted to go by sea. The Carlisle to Lancaster line was extended you see, to include Silloth and Liverpool with this sort of thing in mind.'

"'Excellent my dear Anderson, I would wager you are exactly right. Tell me is there any way we could contact your counterpart at Liverpool to confirm this?'

"'Well they've got one of them new fangled telephone things at the Post Office. We could try there.'

"With that, he showed me the way to the Post Office, where the telephone operator connected me to the Harbourmaster in Liverpool, much to the annoyance of the local Postmaster, who was far from happy with being called from his bed at such an ungodly hour.

"I discovered that our opponents had indeed left, sailing down the Mersey and out into the Irish Sea only this morning. I then compounded the Postmaster's anger by insisting I send a telegram to London."

"To London?" I questioned.

"More work for my dear brother I'm afraid to say," replied Holmes.

"Mycroft? Why not call him when you had access to the telephone?"

"My dear Watson, therein lays a great irony. Whereas I can find and use the most up to date communication facilities in a remote little corner of England, the thought that a telephone would be available in Mycroft's Pall Mall lodgings would be abhorrent to him. As for such a facility in the Diogenes Club, why, half of the members would be in need your professional attention at the mere suggestion! No; the only chance we have is if Mycroft can act quickly at the receipt of my telegram, although I did request he at least *tries* to telephone our hotel at the conclusion of his work."

"What have you asked of him?" I asked.

"All will be revealed later," was my friend's infuriatingly reply, as he rose from our table, after our enjoyable lunch.

With that comment, Holmes shut up as tight as a clam on the subject of the case for the rest of the afternoon. No amount of coaxing from me could make him divulge any further information until around four thirty, when there was a knock on our door and young Billy entered.

"Another telegram from London Mr. Holmes."

"Thank you Billy," said Holmes, rewarding the youngster, once more with a silver coin. Then opening the message, "*Mycroft!*" Holmes virtually sang his brother's name and handed me the paper. It read:

OPERATION SUCCESSFUL STOP WILL BE
RETURNED BEFORE END OF WEEK STOP WILL
CALL LATER WITH DETAILS END

MYCROFT

"Does this mean that the drums will be returned before the end of the week?" I asked.

"It does indeed, my boy!" was Holmes triumphant response.

"So the case is at an end. I must congratulate you Holmes, it looked completely cloudy to me."

"It is not quite over Watson, I have to go out for an hour or so."

With that Holmes left me to fill in the missing pieces of the jigsaw; something – despite ploughing the deepest furrows of my mind, in an effort to cultivate a plausible explanation to the mystery – I found virtually impossible to do.

He returned in a surprisingly downbeat mood later that evening and refused to speak of the case, other than to say, 'I have just received the telephone call from Mycroft as I returned' – the solemnity of his tone was in marked contrast to his earlier mood – 'our work will be concluded tomorrow'.

Once back in the fug of our sitting room, he lit a pipe and threw another log on the fading fire, which immediately retaliated with a loud crackle and a spray of sparks. He sat quietly and gazed into the flames as they roared back into life; an incandescent hue becoming visible in his cheeks after being out in the cold evening air.

For my part, I was weary from my own in-action and I sat nodding in my chair, struggling to fend off the drawing on of sleep. My mind drifted back, in its semi-conscious state, first to Maiwand and my own horrific experiences, and thence to Roman times where my strange dream world had the invaders battling against the advancing Scots, whilst being aided by King Arthur. And yet all the while, throughout my strange hallucinations, I was conscious of the old grandfather clock, on the far side of our sitting room, arduously ticking the hour by.

I was unaware of how much time had passed during my slumber before I was propelled back into consciousness with a startling suddenness; my bizarre dreaming was interrupted by my friend's hand on my shoulder, "Watson? You should turn in, old fellow, we have a busy day ahead of us tomorrow."

Chapter Twelve

The Perpetrator Exposed

In my long and adventurous life that has seen me travel on three continents, serve my country and witness countless adventures with my friend Mr. Sherlock Holmes, there are certain individual days that – although memorable for different reasons – stand out above others.

For example, two days I think of with great fondness are those when my late beloved Mary and latterly, my current dear wife agreed to join in matrimony with me. Another example would be that spring day in 1894, when Holmes turned up in my surgery, after his three-year absence; an event that caused me to faint for the one and only time in my life. A further case in point is the distinct memory I have of that terrible day in June 1880 that saw me involved in the dreadful battle at Maiwand – something that I have recounted elsewhere in this narrative. This in turn brings me back to Tuesday 20th October 1903; another day that, for me, will remain unforgettable.

The day began with my rising to find Holmes dressed and in excited mood, ready no doubt for his extravagant performance at the castle that would see him bring down the curtain on another successful case.

"If the thieves did *not* use the hidden passageways, as I suggested yesterday," I commented during breakfast, "I still cannot see how the drums could have been taken without someone noticing – and for what motive? As for the inference that someone as senior as the Regimental Sergeant Major could somehow be involved – Irish connections or not – is surely impossible."

Holmes rose from the table, clearly not wishing to debate the subject, "Only yesterday you told me that the piece referred to them as being *mythical* passageways. I shall meet you in the Colonel's office in half an hour, Watson, and remember – as I have told you on many occasions – when you eliminate the impossible, whatever remains, however improbable ..."

"Must be the truth," I completed, as my friend walked away.

I finished my breakfast and went back to our rooms to get my hat and coat. Minutes later I was walking through the lobby of our diggings heading for the scene of the case's finale. As I stepped out on to the street I noticed a group of rough looking characters loafing by the town hall steps, opposite. For some reason I was overcome by a feeling of great uneasiness and feared that they were up to no good.

I proceeded down the, by now, well-trodden street towards the castle however, sure in the knowledge that my friend would soon be providing me with another successful case to relay to his many admirers, who so enjoyed reading about his many adventures. From my own point of view, I was also looking forward to seeing the end of the mystery and returning home to my wife.

At the street's end, it meets the cobbled bridge that leads across the moat to the castle itself and it was at this point that I was met by Sergeant Smith of the local constabulary. He was standing there with a smug expression on his face.

"Good morning Doctor, I believe we have a successful conclusion to the case," he said.

"Yes," I rather drew out the word before adding, "thanks to the work of Mr. Holmes, I hope you recognise."

"I suppose credit where it's due," was his foolish reply, "but I don't think even the skilled amateur like Mr. Holmes could be so successful without the guidance of the regular force."

[The scene outside the Castle Gate]

I was saved from prolonging the inane conversation and – as best I could – illustrating Holmes's solitary denouement, by the distinctive sound of a policeman's whistle that came from the direction of the town centre.

"If you'll excuse me Doctor," said Smith, "it seems my services are needed elsewhere."

He set off at pace in the direction of the apparent trouble, while I turned to walk up to the castle. As I did so, the regimental band struck up from its interior. Once under the portcullis and onto the castle square, I discovered that rehearsals were apparently underway for Arroyo Day, that was now just over a week away. To see the soldiers in action and hear the band again brought back rather fonder memories once more of my own, all too brief, military career. As I progressed across the square I could not help myself breaking into a swaggering march in time with the music.

On the opposite side of the square, in the entrance to the Sergeants's Mess, I observed Sergeant Armstrong in deep, animated conversation with his cousin, the Inspector. If it were not for the fact that the men were close relatives, their appearance would have challenged my long held view that soldiers and policemen have always made rather uncomfortable bedfellows. I must repeat however, that I was extremely impressed by both men, and the sentimentalist in me was warmed by how proud their family must be regarding their respective achievements and service to the local community.

I climbed the stairs to Colonel Hulme's first floor office, smiling to myself after my brief stint on the parade ground. "Good morning Lance Corporal," I said addressing young Robins, who was sitting at his desk in the outer office.

"Good morning Doctor," he replied looking up. I sensed something was very wrong by the grave expression on his face and his rather sepulchral tone, "if you would go straight in sir, they are expecting you."

I knocked and entered. The sight that greeted me – and my instant realisation of what I was beholding – came like a hammer blow to the solar plexus, producing a feeling of numbness akin to the similar experience on that other appalling day over ten years earlier, when I stood on the precipice of those terrifying falls at Reichenbach, believing my friend to have fallen to his death.

The Commanding Officer was sitting with his elbows on his desk and his linked fingers forming a single fist under his chin, while his face displayed a mixed expression of shame and disappointment. Holmes was standing, facing the other person in the room. The other person was slouching in a chair opposite Hulme's desk, the very picture of guilt.

Harry Vaughan!

I was paralysed with disbelieve as I stared at the scene before me.

Holmes broke what appeared to be an endless silence. "Come in Watson, the case is at an end."

I could hardly recognise the figure slumped in his chair, a figure I had never seen without a straight back and proud military bearing.

It was Holmes again; "After I left you last evening Watson, I visited Captain Vaughan and appraised him of my findings. When he learned of our successes he decided to do the honourable thing."

"Honourable?" mumbled Colonel Hulme to himself through his bristling moustache.

"I cannot believe it!" I said, rather pathetically, "why?"

Vaughan remained silent, unable to look me in the eye, ashamed and embarrassed by his apparent involvement in the theft.

"I shall explain fully later Watson," said Holmes.

After he had gained some composure, Colonel Hulme instructed Robins to arrange for Vaughan to be placed under house arrest. Some moments later, a party came into the office and marched my former colleague out. This was to be the last time I would ever see my former friend, colleague and saviour.

The colonel this time broke a further uncomfortable silence, "I have asked Inspector Armstrong to join us." He was clearly trying his best to hide his anger and disappointment.

Unknowingly, I moved across the office before my legs collapsed from under me and I slumped into the chair vacated by Vaughan some moments earlier. I sat there in abject disbelief, with the latter half of Holmes's favourite phrase "... whatever remains, must be the truth," ringing around the numb corridors of my mind. My feelings of giddy confusion were compounded by the noise of the regimental band, who continued their rehearsals outside. Far from the crisp, bright military melodies I found myself enjoying only minutes earlier, I now sat there in silence, only vaguely aware of the tuneless, muffled noise that emanated from the square below.

Such was my disbelief that my imagination was clearly playing tricks on me; the one thing seemed so real that morning were the portraits of Colonel Hulme's predecessors that adorned the walls of his office; their proud features appeared to be scowling as they looked down on the shameful scene that befell them.

Although I was aware of the presence of Holmes and Hulme, both of whom had been joined by Inspector Armstrong and Sergeant Smith during this period, I was clearly in no mental state to comprehend what was being said; their lips seemed to be out of synchronization with their voices, that, in my confusion, sounded like a gramophone record that needed winding up. I therefore had to rely on my friend to appraise me on what was said between the four, afterwards.

Holmes told me that he ran through the series of events with the policemen and the C.O., recounting his trip to Silloth and the telegram from his brother Mycroft that confirmed his findings.

"Had it not been for my brother's connections, Colonel," he said, "I am afraid your trophies may never have been recovered. Furthermore, I would not have been able to prove Vaughan's involvement in their theft."

"I am immensely grateful to you *and* your brother Mr. Holmes," replied the senior officer, and then reverted talking almost to himself, "I would never have believed Harry Vaughan would have been involved in such a crime. I trusted the man implicitly," and then re-addressing Holmes, "I wonder what else he has been up to during his time with the regiment?"

"I think we can safely say that Captain Vaughan thought long and hard about his actions. I do not believe he took the decision to participate in the theft lightly and you can rest assured that this was the only blemish on an otherwise flawless career."

"I think it was pretty obvious that it was an inside job," said Sergeant Smith, much to the annoyance of his superior officer.

"Be quiet boy!" rebuked the Inspector, "we would still have been looking for the drums by next Arroyo Day had Mr. Holmes and Doctor Watson not taken over the investigation." Then addressing my friend, Inspector Armstrong said, "I cannot thank you enough Mr. Holmes, not only for your involvement in the stolen drums, but your apprehension of the Adams gang *and* your assistance with Sir Henry's visit last week. I feel the regular force has a lot to learn from you." It was clear that Smith had not yet learned the humility and intelligence displayed by his Inspector.

"Do not mention it, my dear Armstrong," was Holmes's modest reply, "I have enjoyed working with you immensely. It is a pity some of your colleagues do not share your view." His sardonic reply was not lost on those present.

"Will the other members of the gang be returned?" asked the Inspector.

"My brother will arrange their transportation in the next few days."

The colonel then spoke, "You have cleared up this problem Mr. Holmes and I am now confident that the French colours will be returned in time for our celebrations, although we have not much to celebrate this year. The shame on the regiment," he added, again to himself. "But you have done your job Mr. Holmes and for that I add my thanks to that of the Inspector. Please accept this as just reward for your efforts." He handed Holmes an envelope that contained a cheque for his services.

"Thank you Colonel," replied Holmes. "I do not see the need for us to prolong our visit, so if you will excuse us, we shall return to London." Lieutenant Colonel Hulme assented with a silent nod. Holmes then broke my reverie, "Watson? It is time we were leaving."

I looked up, startled, before trying to wrench a monosyllabic affirmation from my chest, but it got stuck in my throat and virtually died on my lips. I was vaguely aware of offering a hand to the Commanding Officer and the senior policeman and we left them to ponder the situation.

Sergeant Smith also excused himself stating that there had been a disturbance at the town hall and he needed to return to 'clear the problem up'.

As Holmes and I descended the stairs, Sergeant Armstrong met us. It was clear by his expression – his face clouded with bewilderment – that he was fully aware of the events of the past few hours and I realised that this is what he and his policeman cousin would have been talking about when I had observed them earlier.

The normally assured tone of the Non Commissioned Officer faltered as he addressed us, "I would have sworn there'd been a mistake but Harry came to see me last night, after you'd seen him Mr. Holmes. He talked me through what had happened. I'm still in a state of shock to be honest."

"Your friend took the honourable way out Sergeant," said Holmes. "He also confessed to your Commanding Officer this morning."

"Yes, he said he was going to; typical 'H', that." Armstrong then looked quizzically, unsure whether or not to contradict himself. It was one of those occasions when one is so sure of something – or someone – that one is thrown into a state of confusion when it is proved that the opposite is true to what one is so sure about. Vaughan's friend and colleague then broached a subject that was clearly bothering him, "Was it me that put you on to Harry, sir?"

"Do not torture yourself unnecessarily," was Holmes's compassionate reply, "all of the evidence and testimonies were suggestive in themselves, but there was no one piece of evidence, given from anyone, which gave excessive weight, one way or another to the investigation. It was not until it was all available and could be pieced together that the true picture of what happened became apparent."

"It explains why the captain asked me to perform the review in Penrith I suppose," said the soldier, through his vacant stare.

"Indeed."

"This chap that Harry was dealing with – he wasn't a shortish, thin bloke with brown collar length hair, was he?"

"He was," replied Holmes.

The NCO growled an imprecation to himself, as he turned away in anger, "I must have been there on one of the nights Vaughany was meeting him in one of the local pubs. We hadn't arranged to meet but it just so happened that I went in for a swift one after work. There's Harry sitting on his own, in the corner of the bar. He looked up and there was such an unusual expression on his face – clearly he wasn't expecting me.

"'Looking for some company?' I said.

"'Geordie! I'm … er … here to meet someone.'

"'Sounds a bit cloak and dagger! Hope you're not up to anything untoward,' I said jokingly.

"Now I think back, Harry laughed nervously at this comment and looked around furtively, 'No, no, just a bit of private business,' he replied.

"We talked for a while but I can see now that he was on edge the whole time. I finally made my excuses and left after having a drink with him. As I left the bar, the bloke I've just described passed me on his way into the pub. With nothing more than a reflex glance, I looked through the window of the pub from the street outside, as I walked past. Sure enough there was this bloke shaking hands with 'H' before sitting down with him.

"My God! It's all so clear to me now looking back. If only I'd known what the bugger's motives were," continued Armstrong, "I could have gone back in and brought Harry to his senses. I would've shown that la'al sod a thing or two an 'all."

"You could not have possibly known what was occurring that night," said Holmes, "I'm sure Captain Vaughan is well aware that he has a trusted friend and colleague. He acted in full knowledge of the possible consequences however, so I repeat, Sergeant, there is no need to torture yourself over the matter."

"Do you think that his otherwise immaculate record will count in his favour?" The question was at best naive, as the soldier would have had a greater knowledge of such military procedures than Holmes. It was clear that, like me, he was not thinking straight and had resorted to clutching at straws, on his friend's behalf.

"I have little knowledge on how the army deals with such matters," confirmed the detective. "We must leave now, Sergeant Armstrong. Thank you once again for your help and good luck."

We shook hands with the crestfallen NCO, who was still unable to hide his disappointment and shock – something that I could easily relate to. Given the surprisingly speedy conclusion to the case, Holmes suggested we attempt to catch the ten forty-five train heading for the capital.

Back at The Crown and Mitre, our witnessing of the aftermath of what Sergeant Smith had referred to as 'a disturbance' completed our surreal morning. Apparently the gang of ruffians I had seen hanging around the town hall steps had been waiting for some of the city's dignitaries to arrive. It was their job to complete the laying of tramlines throughout the city centre and it appears they were in dispute over payment; hence their protest.

We entered the lobby to see Mrs. Graham dabbing the grazed forehead of the unfortunate Town Hall Doorman, Mr. Wilson, as his battered topper lay on the floor beside him.

[Carlisle Citadel Station from where we returned home]

Sergeant Smith was interviewing Mr. Graham and noting down his responses, "So you saw what happened Sam?"

"Oh aye, it was a rare ole barney!" was our host's enthusiastic reply. "Old Mr. Wilson there cem down the steps to move them along. Things then got a bit ugly and a couple of your lads who were walkin' up Scotch Street moved in. Then it really kicked off; knocking seven bells out of each other the' were. That's when one of the coppers whistled for help. I think you know the rest."

On the street outside a group of uniformed policemen were in the process of preparing to frogmarch the individuals arrested back down Scotch Street to the police station.

This bizarre scene only added to my state of dumfoundedness. Holmes and I left the official forces to deal with the situation and went up to our rooms to prepare for our journey home. I packed my things in silence, as the echo of banging draws and cupboard doors permeated from my friend's lamentably untidy room. Billy once more helped us with our luggage and when in the lobby of the Inn once more, Mr. Graham informed us that Colonel Hulme had already made preparations to settle our expenses. We thanked him and his wife for their hospitality and left in the carriage he had ordered for us.

At the railway station, all noises seemed to merge with the muffled messages from the tannoy announcer; such was my mindset. Holmes appreciated my state of shock and allowed me time to regain my poise before explaining the case. I was virtually oblivious as our train gently rattled out of the border city and headed south into the idyllic parkland of the Lake District.

Chapter Thirteen

The Case Unravelled

I sat staring blankly out of the carriage window at the dark clouds that hung menacingly in the sky like enormous muslin sacks, ready to discharge their cargo on the area below at any moment.

"I just cannot believe it," I mumbled to myself for the umpteenth time and then, finally directing a question at Holmes, "why would Harry Vaughan do such a thing?"

"For money!" he replied. "Captain Vaughan would have reached his retirement within the next two years having completed thirty years service. And what had he to show for it? Not even a Majority. Did it not strike you as odd when he contacted you, that in the many years since you went your separate ways, had only achieved one promotion?"

If I had to choose one lesson from working with Holmes for so long, it would have to be that there is only one thing worse than other people's stupidity – and that is one's own! "I must confess, I did not pick up on that at the time," I said, annoyed, once more, at my own dimwittedness.

"No? Still, you must not be so hard on your friend Watson; I view him as a victim in all this sorry mess. The man as you quite rightly pointed out was a fearless soldier but the truth is that Vaughan is a maverick who did not tow the party line, so to speak. A classic example of this was his saving of yourself all those years ago. Did you not recount to me that he '… led a group of soldiers out from behind the lines', to save Murray and yourself? What you considered brave, his superiors viewed as foolhardy.

"Then there was Sergeant Armstrong's comment that he had to reign his more senior colleague back from '... running out, all guns blazing'. The truth of the matter is Watson that this man was popular with his subordinates but much of his work went unrecognised by his superiors. You yourself, described his as 'ambitious', and yet it appears his ambitions were never realised. This evidently led to resentment and his attempting to secure a nest egg for his forthcoming retirement."

"But how were you alerted to him?" I asked.

"If the truth be told, I suspected something was amiss before we even left Baker Street. Vaughan stated that he knew you no longer lived in our rooms through your writings in *The Strand*. Why then did he send his letter to Baker Street, knowing full well that you would not be there to receive it? Furthermore, why would he send a letter at all? Surely a telegram would be in order given the lack of time before the 28th.

"When we interviewed Robins he told us that, contrary to what we were led to believe, it was not Vaughan at all who suggested to his Commanding Officer that we could help. It was Robins *himself* who planted the seed with Hulme after recalling his brother witnessed our solving of the Colonel Barclay affair some years ago. *Armstrong* then commented that Vaughan knew you. At no time during the week of the theft did Vaughan recommend our help, until prompted, this despite his acknowledgment to us – in the presence of the colonel – that the resources of the local constabulary were stretched.

"Then upon our arrival, he met us at the station and then dined with us later; but not only did he fail to protest at my suggestion that we start our investigation the following day, he did not mention the case once during the evening. You obviously did not notice as you were wrapped up in re-living former adventures but I thought it strange, at best.

"Further evidence was submitted by Sergeant Armstrong, who informed us that it was usually his superiors who went out to Penrith to hold the review session, but on this occasion, Vaughan asked him to go. In so doing he conveniently removed a potentially helpful witness from our investigation for a day or so, and this bought his colleagues more time to make their escape. Armstrong himself picked up on this point less than an hour ago, when we spoke with him.

"In short, the whole series of events reeked of delay Watson, and the longer the delay, the greater chance of his confederates completing the theft and making their flight, whilst all the time the trail was going cold. Once they were overseas, there would have been nothing to link Vaughan to the theft."

"Now you mention it," I said, "I dined with him on Sunday night and he never mentioned the case then either, despite originally telling me that the colonel wanted to know the latest position."

"I suspect his visit was prompted by his own nervousness," commented Holmes, before continuing. "Another anomaly came to light when our friend Mr. Scott made reference to his picking up five uniforms to clean, excluding the set he himself replaced in the middle of the week. This after Armstrong had stated that the officers and NCOs used three each. Hulme, Vaughan and Armstrong should have therefore used nine uniforms between them – Scott only dealt with eight. A minor point at the time but suggestive in itself. The sergeant also commented about the dirty uniforms found during his inspection. These men could not possibly dirty their own uniforms when they were twenty miles away! Vaughan must have replaced them after his associates used them."

"Do you know who his associates were?"

"Although I deduced their nationality, I did not learn of their identity until I spoke with Mycroft yesterday. I suspected that the 'Sinn Feine' note we received at the Inn was an effort to side-track us, but it would have been remiss of me not to follow it up."

"So it was Vaughan who sent us the note. Why would he do this?" I asked, still confused.

"As I told yourself and Inspector Armstrong last week, the erstwhile London villains, Styles and Bennett, read of the theft of the drums and saw it as an opportunity to distract the police, thus enabling them to attempt to break-out Adams. But it was not only the Londoners who benefited from their theft at the town hall. Vaughan could not have believed his luck at the opportunist theft, as this muddied the waters still further and gave his colleagues extra time to escape. When I deduced the reason for the second theft, you will recall that before we left the police station, Inspector Armstrong said he would contact the colonel. In doing so – via Hulme – he inadvertently alerted Vaughan to our success, who then acted quickly in an attempt to lead us away from the trail once more, by making the Irish suggestion."

"That's right" – I snapped my fingers in sudden recollection – "we left Armstrong to go to the prison and then returned to the Inn where the note was waiting for us."

"As it was, our trip to the Irish quarter helped us enormously, for I must confess I did not anticipate stumbling into the same public house as Vaughan and his colleagues had frequented shortly before the robbery. In trying to lead us away from our path, he in fact, carelessly drew us nearer our goal.

"You will recall upon our visit to the Irish pub that the landlord told us of the strangers, two weeks earlier? My reason for returning to the bar as we were leaving was to describe the gentleman that joined the group. The landlord confirmed my description of Captain Vaughan. Furthermore, he added that the description actually fitted another man in the group; 'I thought they were brothers', he told me. Vaughan was actually meeting his associates to finalise their plan for the following week. The choice of location was obviously because of its close proximity to the castle, as was the other location for the separate meeting between Vaughan and the leader of the gang, alluded to by Sergeant Armstrong earlier.

"Back at the 'Joiner's Arms', the landlord told us that only Vaughan and one other appeared to be conversing, during this insidious meeting. The reason for this was that the other members of the gang could not speak English! You see Watson, Vaughan's associates were not Irish, but French!"

"French?" I ejaculated.

"Special agents, working for the French 34eme Regiment, which brings us to the motive for the theft. They were plotting to recapture their drums, lost all those years ago in Spain. You are the military man Watson not I, but the purpose of my first telegram to Mycroft last Friday was to request his services; by making some discrete enquiries through his contacts at the War Office as to the history of our French cousins.

"He established that the regiment in question was founded by Napoleon himself, when he became Emperor in 1804 – raised as a crack outfit, specifically to fight in the seemingly endless campaigns against his European neighbours. They did not get off to a very auspicious start however, with our friends from Cumberland stealing their Drums and Colours on the Spanish Peninsular.

"Things went from bad to worse as your military history will tell you, my friend. The only successful campaign the French took part in, in the whole of the century just past, was when they were allied to Britain in the Crimea. Alas the 34eme were not part of the French forces in Russia. This therefore begs the question – upon their centenary – what do they have to celebrate?"

"So they thought that they would restore some credibility by retrieving the trophies lost by their fallen comrades," I concluded.

"Precisely," cried Holmes, "but to do so, they needed an insider who had access to keys and equipment. In the frustrated Vaughan, they found the perfect accessory, who brought the number of the gang to five."

"So why did you keep referring to the possible involvement of RSM McCue?"

"Watson, I did not; *you* did! Once you heard of McCue's Irish connections, your imagination took over once more and

– given his rather strange behaviour and the coincidental timing of his arrival with that of the theft – you automatically assumed that he was somehow involved."

"But if that is the case," I protested, "why did you question Hulme about Young and McCue and not Vaughan?"

"Simply to eliminate them from our enquiries. I was already convinced of Vaughan's activities, but I need to satisfy myself that there was no other involvement from within the regiment.

"My second telegram to Mycroft again requested his help by using his influence at the War Office and with the Admiralty. He organised the despatching of a frigate from Plymouth – they were therefore intercepted and subsequently arrested the French members of the gang as they attempted to make it across the Channel.

"During my conversation with Mycroft later, he appraised me of another little gem. He informed me that the leader of the gang was none other than my old adversary Serge Bazin. Clearly he specialises in bold, high profile, outrageous thefts, as it was Bazin who was the main operative behind the attempted theft of the Mona Lisa during the early months of '91. You may recall I spent some time working for the French government at the time and succeeded in thwarting the attempt.

"He was, of course, one of the late Professor Moriarty's many foreign agents and the whole episode was the prelude to our ill fated continental sojourn later that spring. Unlike his three colleagues, he is fluent in English and it was he who made the trip up to Carlisle some months ago.

"When I confronted Vaughan last evening he admitted that Bazin approached him earlier this year and proposed the daring raid. Having an air of confidence himself, not to mention his command of the language, he fitted in comfortably to the military environment. Vaughan told me that the Frenchman scoured the drinking haunts of the local soldiers and finally struck lucky when he befriended the solitary Vaughan in one of his more reflective moods.

"You may remember that Sergeant Armstrong informed us that he and his colleagues felt Vaughan was '... unlucky to be pipped for the Major's job", by Young. The captain made the mistake of divulging this information to the devious Bazin and the latter played upon the 'mistreatment' Vaughan had received from the army during his long and loyal service. In doing so, he snared the vulnerable officer and convinced him that the plan to steal the drums would benefit them both financially.

"He and Vaughan then planned the operation for the week when key personnel would be training with their part time colleagues. This would also clear Vaughan himself, of any suspicion, as he would be accompanying his Commanding Officer. Once Bazin knew that he had the local help he had sought, he returned to France and carefully selected the personnel for the job. As you are aware by now, another key member of the group was the one who could pass for Vaughan himself. The other two were simply hired muscle."

"So how was the theft committed when Vaughan was not there to supervise it?" I still could not follow.

"Through sheer bravado my boy!" replied my friend with a flourish. "Vaughan had gone through the layout of the castle with Bazin and briefed him on the lack of security during the night. During my inspection of the keyhole to the storeroom door, I observed several minute metal shavings, lying loose in the base of the barrel. These, I suspected were created by the burring of a new key in the lock. Vaughan obviously had access to keys and again he confirmed this when I spoke with him. He told me that he had keys cut from the originals for his French associates to use on the night of the robbery.

"He had then taken the spare uniforms of the soldiers who accompanied him to Penrith and issued one of his own uniforms to the member of the gang who matched his build and appearance – hence his use of only two uniforms whilst in Penrith. His look-a-like obviously led the robbery on the night, posing as the absent captain with his associates masquerading as private soldiers of the Border Regiment.

"The adverse weather on the night in question clearly concerned Vaughan. You may recall that Armstrong told us that his friend and colleague left the field with the injured Yeomanry Officer during the training exercise and that Vaughan failed to return for some hours? The latter told me that he used the opportunity to contact Bazin to check on the latest position.

"What about the unfortunate guard, Walker, do you think they intended to kill him?" I asked.

"I do not believe for a moment that this was part of the original plan, things simply spiralled out of control" – Holmes adopted a more solemn tone - "judging by the evidence given by Nixon, upon finding his colleague, I suspect that the gang intended to slip into the castle while the guard went to freshen up, no doubt surprising him from behind before gagging and blindfolding him. Either they mis-timed their attack or Walker turned and saw them, because Nixon claimed there was a pool of blood some yards from the block and then a trial that led into the building. I suggest they beat him and then dragged him into the garderobe block, leaving him for dead. The poor man – semi-conscious – commendably attempted to crawl back out and raise the alarm."

"That explains the position of his body when Nixon found him," I completed.

"When we visited Walker in hospital, Nixon assumed that he was calling for his wife as he picked out the 'CH' sound. It is my belief that Walker was actually trying to pronounce the letter 'H' – one of Vaughan's many nicknames amongst his subordinates – as his fleeting glance of the villains on the night in question, may well have resulted in him mistaking the gang member for Captain Vaughan.

"Incidentally, isn't it strange?" – Holmes digressed – "If you recall, during our very first investigation together, our old friend Inspector Lestrade made a similar mistake involving that particular woman's Christian name.

"Although I repeat, I do not believe their intention was to hurt anyone, once Walker had discovered them, they had little choice but to incapacitate him and progress with the

162

burglary. Even if Walker did recover and claim that Vaughan had been involved in the crime, the captain would have had a cast-iron alibi, as he was with his commanding officer all the time. Walker's claim would surely have been put down to his head injury.

"Once the Frenchmen had possession of the crates, containing the drums, from the store room, they brazenly rode out of the front gate on the assumption that – even if spotted in the poor light – no one would challenge Captain Vaughan and his men as they apparently took some previously forgotten supplies to the training camp. And so it proved as they made clean away with the Border Regiment's most treasured possessions."

"They then took the crates containing their booty to Silloth from where they sailed back to France?" I ventured.

"Excellent Watson! But this is where fate leant a hand. They *intended* to sail from Silloth but as we now know, the storm scuppered their plans and their boat was wrecked, so Bazin was forced to make other arrangements. Mycroft confirmed what we already knew; that as his colleagues stayed with the drums in the warehouse, the leader left to organise another boat to meet them in Liverpool, from where they would sail for home. Further time was lost however, as the replacement vessel was not only a slower sailing ship, as opposed to their original steamer, but it had to sail from the southern port of Marseilles. Although we were ignorant of the fact at the time, this protracted delay bought us the time we needed to recapture the trophies."

For the rest of our journey I sat in silence, trying to take in the adventure we had just experienced; the intrigue, the daring and above all else, the ultimate betrayal by my former friend and colleague. As with so many of the battles won through the bestial savagery, in the recent Great War, I viewed Holmes's success as a Pyrrhic victory.

Upon our arrival at Euston, Holmes and I shared a hansom to Baker Street, from where I needed to pick up some papers, that I had left on my last visit, prior to my returning home.

Asking the driver to wait, I politely declined Mrs. Hudson's kind offer of supper and followed Holmes up to my former quarters. I picked up my things and turned to leave.

"Until next time then, old man!" I said, turning to leave.

"There won't be a next time," was Holmes's matter-of-fact reply, "I am retiring."

[*The safely recovered Arroyo Drums*]

I stopped in my tracks, dumbfounded at what I had just heard. "What? You are joking surely?"

"On the contrary my friend, I have decided the time has come to step down from this great stage of crime. I have considered the matter for some time and was going to tell you when you called the other day, with news of this case. I knew I could not let down my loyal friend and chronicler, so I postponed informing you of my decision. I will be moving to Sussex to keep bees."

"*Sussex? Bees?*" For the second time that day I was rooted to the spot, thunderstruck with disbelief.

"Calm yourself Watson," said my friend, putting a hand on my shoulder, "I *have* spoke of retirement in the past."

"Yes, but I never thought you were serious!" I said, sounding I'm sure like a schoolboy who has had his catapult confiscated. "You still have so much to offer!"

"As kind as ever old friend, but I'm afraid I cannot agree. You need go no further than this most recent of cases to see that my powers are diminishing; I have been sluggish in thought and slow on the uptake, relying on good fortune and bad weather to assist me in solving the mystery.

"No; we all have to hang up our stethoscopes and magnifying glasses sometime, Watson, and I believe my time has arrived. Now, you should return to your wife and I will keep you informed of my whereabouts."

I returned home and spent the rest of the week completing my writing of the case, admittedly, still in somewhat of a daze after the revelations of the Tuesday just passed.

When it came to putting Holmes's cases into print, he and I had a strict understanding. Whenever my friend advised me of a case he did not wish me to publish, or when either of us felt it was not in the interest of the public or certain individuals to make a case known, I would – upon the completion of its writing – tie it up with a black ribbon, before placing it in my old despatch box. This would act as an instant indicator to myself when, months or even years later, I would delve into my hoard with view to contacting my literary agents at *The Strand*, who would then, with the assistance of Mr. Paget's marvellous illustrations, make known one of my friend's many adventures.

With this particular case, I took it upon myself to class it as one of the adventures that should go without publication, as I felt great discomfort at the thought of highlighting the misdemeanours of a former friend and colleague, who I once liked and admired tremendously. I simply marked the cover sheet 'Spanish Drums', took a strip of the aforementioned ribbon, tied it quite deliberately and made sure it went to the very bottom of the box containing my written work.

And so ended the final case conducted by Mr. Sherlock Holmes of 221B Baker Street. Of course it did not prove to be the end of his magnificent career, as various clients have called him out of retirement over the past years, to look into their problems; some of which, as I recall, he has investigated while using his old lodgings as his London base.

The French gang were returned to Carlisle where they were charged with theft and the attempted murder of Private Walker. As for Harry Vaughan, I heard that he received a dishonourable discharge from the army and returned to his hometown of Reading, a broken man.

Epilogue

Several years later I had call to accompany my dear wife and her sister on short break in the Lake District. Although travelling north towards Cumberland instantly brought back sad memories of my previous visit to that part of the country, I did not dwell on them. That was until one morning when I was reading the local paper in the hotel over breakfast. There was a piece about the forthcoming 'Arroyo Day' at Carlisle Castle. Until that point the significance of the time of year, and the coincidence of our visit had not properly dawned on me. As my wife and sister-in-law had made other arrangements for the 28th October, I asked their permission to excuse myself and take the train through to Carlisle to witness the celebration of the anniversary of the regiment's famous action.

The train pulled into the station and I experienced mixed emotions, as the expectation of witnessing the regiment's celebration was tinged with sadness, as the full recollection of my previous visit came flooding back to me.

I decided to walk to the castle, given that it was a pleasant afternoon. Leaving the station, I walked across the large natural courtyard area where we had witness the arrival of the Liberal Party leader. As I past the County Gaol and City Arms public house, I smiled to myself as I recalled how Holmes and I – incognito – had initiated our entrapment of the remaining members of the Adams gang. Further along English Street young Billy's words came back to me, when he told us about his father's Inn and how it was going to be '... rebuilt as the county's top hotel', following its demolition. Indeed the sight that beheld me was an impressive one; the renamed Crown and Mitre Hotel was a most elegant building. I could not resist entering, not only to admire the ornate decor, but also to see if Mr. & Mrs. Graham and their son, who made us so welcome, were still there. Alas, there was no sign of the former occupants and the uniformed doorman told me that he did not know where they had gone.

*[The renamed Crown and Mitre Hotel
was a most elegant building]*

The magnificent castle was just as I had remembered it and many locals were making their way under the portcullis, as I approached. Inside, on the edge of the square, temporary grandstands had been erected for spectators of the imminent parade. I decided on a suitable spot from which to witness the regiment and was about to climb onto the gangway of the grandstand when a voice called out from behind me.

"Doctor Watson? Doctor Watson, is that you?"

I turned to find none other than the man Holmes had described as '... probably the most honourable and trustworthy man in the regiment', and who had helped Holmes tremendously in his solving of the case.

"Sergeant Armstrong!" I replied with genuine delight.

"Lieutenant now sir," said the soldier offering a hand.

"Congratulations!" I said, not having noticed the markings on his tunic, "and very well deserved too."

"Thank you sir, what brings you back to Carlisle?"

"Oh, I am just on holiday with my wife, in the lakes, and I thought I would take advantage of the opportunity of enjoying 'Arroyo Day' – something Mr. Holmes and I never had the chance to do the last time we visited."

"Well it's very nice to see you, Doctor. How is Mr. Holmes doing?"

"He's fine. After we returned to London he moved down to Sussex where he keeps his bees! Although I do not see as much of him as I would like, I know he still keeps his detective hat on by accepting the odd case.

"Speaking of detectives, how is your cousin, the Inspector?"

"Yes, old Corny's still going strong. Still regularly talks about his encounter with Mr. Holmes, I'll tell him you were asking after him."

Armstrong invited me to join him in the VIPs box. We spoke at length on how life had treated us both since our last meeting and simultaneously bowed our heads in sadness when the name of our mutual former comrade came up. Without discussing the matter at length it was clear that we shared a common view; whereas we recognised his crime, we still remembered Vaughan as a valued friend and colleague.

[*The Arroyo Day celebrations*]

The parade itself consisted of a young Drum Major and four drummer-boys, all of whom were in period dress from the Napoleonic Wars. They in turn were followed by the modern day corps of drummers with the regimental band following on behind, keeping the crowds entertained with some classic military tunes. In watching the soldiers carrying the drums and colours, it occurred to me that this was the first time I had actually seen the items that we recovered those years earlier. Even though it was a dull October afternoon, the highly polished brass barrels of the drums – that were tipped along the upper and lower rim with the colours of the French tricolour – glinted proudly, as the bandsmen marched past.

There was then a brief re-enactment of how the drums were captured, carried out by members of the regiment, again in period uniform. Afterward there was an address by the Commanding Officer. Lieutenant Colonel Hulme had retired some years earlier, but the new man obviously shared his predecessor's pride in the drums and the significance of the day they were celebrating. Speaking with great gusto, he informed his men and the crowd that this was the most important day in the regiment's calendar and how '... they, and the City, should be proud of the regiment's achievements to date'.

Thinking back to this event, there now seems to be a certain innocence about his address, given that a few years later, the regiment – along with soldiers from all over the world – would be involved in a war we hope will end all wars.

I must say however, that I enjoyed the parade tremendously, notwithstanding the sad memories produced at the thought of our absent friend.

"Please tell Mr. Holmes I was asking after him," said Lieutenant Armstrong as we wished each other farewell, at the completion of the afternoon's celebration. I returned to my wife and her sister and carried on our most relaxing holiday.

We returned to London shortly thereafter and, when my circumstances allowed me, I made a point of visiting Holmes at his bee-keeping farm, to inform him of my visit to Carlisle and pass on the regards offered to him by Lieutenant Armstrong. My friend was interested little in the regimental parade but said, with a laconic shrug, "I am pleased to see Armstrong is receiving the reward and advancement that was less forthcoming to your former colleague."

Historical Note

The Arroyo dos Molinos Battle Honour is unique to the Regiment and is a central part of their History and tradition. Dr. Watson's brief account of the Battle itself is an accurate one. It was a successful operation, wreaking havoc on the enemy with very little loss to the allies. In addition there was the remarkable coincidence of the 34th Regiments of the British and French Armies meeting on the battlefield; the British 34th capturing the Drum-Major's Staff and six Drums of the French 34th.

For more than a hundred and thirty years the 34th (Cumberland) Regiment and its successors – from 1881 the 1st Battalion Border Regiment and from 1959 the 1st Battalion The King's Own Royal Border Regiment – have celebrated Arroyo Day. Originally the Drums and Staff were just displayed and later they were trooped as part of a formal parade.

The first record of them is a photograph taken in 1866 and the first recorded use of them was at the presentation of New Colours to the 34th Foot in 1871, when the French Drums and Staff were placed with the Battalion Drums in the centre of the hollow square. The earliest record of the French Drums being paraded is a photograph taken at Crownhill Barracks, Plymouth on Arroyo Day during the first decade of the 20th century, when the Drums and Drum-Major's Staff were carried by the Corps of Drums wearing their normal scarlet

173

full-dress uniforms. On 28th October 1911, the 1st Battalion celebrated the centenary of the Battle with a formal parade, sports activities, balls in the Officers' and Sergeant's Messes and a torchlight tattoo. The magnificent photograph at the very beginning of this book is of the gate of Carlisle Castle – which housed the Regimental Depot – on Arroyo Day 1911.

It is not until Arroyo Day 1920 that the first written reference to the parading of the French Drums appears in the 1st Battalion's Digest of Service; this was done during the interval of the sports activities. Six drummer boys dressed in replica drummer's uniforms of the British 34th Foot carried the French Drums and another dressed as the 34th's Drum-Major carried the French Drum-Major's Staff in the post of honour at the head of Regimental Band and Drums on parade. Ever since – whenever possible – it has been the custom on Arroyo Day and on other Regimental occasions to parade the Drums and Staff; these now being carried by soldiers of the Regiment.

Further details about the Battle of Arroyo; the Peninsular War, of which it was part, as well as the countless other campaigns that have seen the Regiment's involvement, can be found at the Border and King's Own Royal Border Regimental Museum in Carlisle Castle, that is open to the public year round. Amongst the vast amount of valuable items and memorabilia from three hundred years of campaigning are the six Arroyo Drums themselves. Also displayed are the medals of Sergeant Moses Simpson, who wrenched the French Drum Major's staff from him during the battle.

Some of the characters in the novel actually existed, such as Isaac Scott, Robert Gibson and Sir Henry Campbell-Bannerman. Others however did not and the fictitious character of Harry Vaughan should not be confused with that of Major Charles Davies Vaughan DSO, hero of the Regiment during the same period. Nor should Lieutenant-Colonel Richard Hulme be mistaken for one of the distinguished Hume family; several of whose members served the Regiment with honour and two of whom – brothers John and Robert

Hume – both commanded units of the Regiment in the 19th century.

There are almost inevitably liberties taken in the novel with regard to certain geographical locations, such as the interior castle buildings and the police station, but it is hoped that local experts will forgive this, as our fictional heroes must be humoured during their adventures.

Martin Daley

If you enjoyed this book then you will be pleased to know that Cornelius Armstrong will return in two new adventures by Martin Daley.

The Casebook of Inspector Armstrong Volume I

Cornelius Armstrong, the Carlisle Inspector who assisted Holmes in this adventure, takes centre stage in the first volume of his own investigations. In *The Italian Murder*, Armstrong investigates the death of a young immigrant in 1903, only to find his enquiries unravel a far wider web of underworld crime. The second short novel, *King Edward's Ghost* sees the detective drawn into a mystery that takes us back six hundred years to the death of Edward I on Burgh Marsh.

For more information about books by Martin Daley visit www.martindaley.co.uk or for those interested in more Sherlock Holmes adventures www.crime4u.com.

"With five volumes you could fill that gap on that second shelf"
(Sherlock Holmes, *The Empty House*)

So why not collect all 42 murder mysteries from Baker Street Studios? Available from all good bookshops, or direct from the publisher with free UK postage & packing at just £7.50 each. Alternatively you can get full details of all our publications, including our range of audio books, and order on-line where you can also join our mailing list and see our latest special offers.

IN THE DEAD OF WINTER
MYSTERY OF A HANSOM CAB
SHERLOCK HOLMES AND THE ABBEY SCHOOL MYSTERY
SHERLOCK HOLMES AND THE ADLER PAPERS
SHERLOCK HOLMES AND THE BAKER STREET DOZEN
SHERLOCK HOLMES AND THE BOULEVARD ASSASSIN
SHERLOCK HOLMES AND THE CHILFORD RIPPER
SHERLOCK HOLMES AND THE CHINESE JUNK AFFAIR
SHERLOCK HOLMES AND THE CIRCUS OF FEAR
SHERLOCK HOLMES AND THE DISAPPEARING PRINCE
SHERLOCK HOLMES AND THE DISGRACED INSPECTOR
SHERLOCK HOLMES AND THE EGYPTIAN HALL ADVENTURE
SHERLOCK HOLMES AND THE FRIGHTENED GOLFER
SHERLOCK HOLMES AND THE GIANT'S HAND
SHERLOCK HOLMES AND THE GREYFRIARS SCHOOL MYSTERY
SHERLOCK HOLMES AND THE HAMMERFORD WILL
SHERLOCK HOLMES AND THE HOLBORN EMPORIUM
SHERLOCK HOLMES AND THE HOUDINI BIRTHRIGHT
SHERLOCK HOLMES AND THE LONGACRE VAMPIRE
SHERLOCK HOLMES AND THE MAN WHO LOST HIMSELF
SHERLOCK HOLMES AND THE MORPHINE GAMBIT
SHERLOCK HOLMES AND THE SANDRINGHAM HOUSE MYSTERY
SHERLOCK HOLMES AND THE SECRET MISSION
SHERLOCK HOLMES AND THE SECRET SEVEN
SHERLOCK HOLMES AND THE TANDRIDGE HALL MYSTERY
SHERLOCK HOLMES AND THE TELEPHONE MURDER MYSTERY
SHERLOCK HOLMES AND THE THEATRE OF DEATH
SHERLOCK HOLMES AND THE THREE POISONED PAWNS
SHERLOCK HOLMES AND THE TITANTIC TRAGEDY
SHERLOCK HOLMES AND THE TOMB OF TERROR
SHERLOCK HOLMES AND THE YULE-TIDE MYSTERY
SHERLOCK HOLMES: A DUEL WITH THE DEVIL
SHERLOCK HOLMES AT THE RAFFLES HOTEL
SHERLOCK HOLMES AT THE VARIETIES
SHERLOCK HOLMES ON THE WESTERN FRONT
SHERLOCK HOLMES: THE GHOST OF BAKER STREET
SPECIAL COMMISSION
THE CASE OF THE MISSING STRADIVARIUS*
THE ELEMENTARY CASES OF SHERLOCK HOLMES
THE TORMENT OF SHERLOCK HOLMES
THE TRAVELS OF SHERLOCK HOLMES
WATSON'S LAST CASE

* HARDBACK AT £15.99

Baker Street Studios Limited, Endeavour House, 170 Woodland Road,
Sawston, Cambridge CB22 3DX
www.breesebooks.com, sales@breesebooks.com

Lightning Source UK Ltd.
Milton Keynes UK
29 November 2010

163646UK00001B/140/P